The muzzle-suppressed guns whistled again, three shots in quick succes̶ the rooftop vibrate ̶ ̶avel shrapnel stung ̶ ̶ but never lost sight ̶ ̶ of an airshaft. Belo̶ ̶ ̶neatly intersecting cross-braces. She took a deep breath as the opening came closer.

This was going to hurt.

"Halt!" the man ordered again.

One last footstep took her over the shaft's edge. Her right hand drew the grappling hook from beneath her jumpsuit. In the single, transcendent instant as lateral motion was joined by vertical drop, she eyed the shaft's cross-braces. She angled her body like a diver and plunged between them. As the two metal beams passed though her field of view, she cast the hook. It caught and held.

Sydney fell into the gloom. The dirty brick shaft lining slid past her more and more rapidly, and air whistled in her ears. A whining sound came from her descent harness as cable unwound. Time seemed to slow as floors passed, one after another.

This was *really* going to hurt

Also available from

SIMON SPOTLIGHT ENTERTAINMENT

ALIAS™

THE
apo™
SERIES

TWO OF A KIND?

FAINA

ALIAS™

THE

SERIES

COLLATERAL DAMAGE

ALIAS™

THE
apo™
SERIES

COLLATERAL DAMAGE

PIERCE ASKEGREN

An original novel based on the

hit TV series created by J. J. Abrams

SⓈE

SIMON SPOTLIGHT ENTERTAINMENT

New York   London   Toronto   Sydney

SSE

SIMON SPOTLIGHT ENTERTAINMENT
An imprint of Simon & Schuster
1230 Avenue of the Americas, New York, New York 10020
Text and cover art copyright © 2005 by Touchstone Television
All rights reserved, including the right of reproduction in whole or in part in any form.
SIMON SPOTLIGHT ENTERTAINMENT and related logo are trademarks of Simon & Schuster, Inc.
Manufactured in the United States of America
First Edition 10 9 8 7 6 5 4 3 2 1
Library of Congress Control Number 2004117772
ISBN 1-4169-0247-3

This book is dedicated to my good friends John Garcia and Erik Morrison, with thanks for their long years of encouragement and support.

Special thanks to my editor, Patrick Price, and my agent, Jennifer Jackson, for help and guidance.

CHAPTER 1

WASHINGTON, D.C.

Ten stories above the streets, visibility was very good, but the air smelled of automobile exhaust and was sticky with summer heat. Not even the breeze that drifted sluggishly though the summer sky helped. Sydney Bristow, atop the tallest commercial structure in the nation's capital, felt the cheap polyester uniform of a commercial equipment maintenance service cling greasily to her skin.

Sweat trickled along the smooth skin of her brow and then dripped into her eyes, where it stung. She brushed the errant droplets aside, blinked, and then refocused on her work.

The weathered air conditioner's housing was industrial-gauge sheet steel. Similar metal boxes lined rooftops around the world. The uniqueness of this particular unit was its location, offering unobstructed line-of-sight access to a building owned by a lobbying company that was a front for Russian Intelligence. The AC unit was a perfect mounting place for the camouflaged remote surveillance device that another agent had earlier bolted to its side.

Sydney entered a series of numbers on what looked like a cell phone. The palm-size device fed commands along a cable connected to the surveillance unit. Forty seconds passed, and then the ersatz phone's display flashed red.

"Download failed," Sydney said into her headset comm-link. "I'm going to try again."

"Negative, Phoenix." The voice was Dixon's. Her longtime field partner was circling the block in a utility van, its doors bearing the same logo as Sydney's uniform. "We go to fallback. Pull the unit."

"One more time, Outrigger," Sydney replied.

She keyed the pseudo-phone again, and nodded as it presented new information. "Diagnostics run okay. The new operating system should—"

"Pull the unit," Dixon said. Ordinarily, he was almost infinitely patient, but now, he sounded ever so slightly irritated. "I can't drive around the block forever without attracting attention."

Sydney sighed very softly. She pressed a final key and set the device aside, but left the connection in place. Reaching into one of her jumpsuit's pockets, she withdrew a slender leather toolkit and extracted a miniature wrench.

"I don't wish to come back up here," she said. From what she had been told, aligning and focusing the unit had been tedious work. She didn't want to repeat the process for a replacement.

"Neither do I, but if it failed the first three times, it's not going to work the fourth, either," Dixon said, then took a deep breath. He sounded patient again, but deliberately so. "Pull the unit. I've got Merlin in my other ear, and he wants to check it in person."

The surveillance unit was impressively well-disguised, installed in housing that resembled an external thermostat. Sydney had already removed the cover. Now, she methodically unbolted the interior apparatus, which was about the size of a deck of cards. The disguising shell could stay behind, both to make her extraction less obvious and, ultimately, to hold the unit's replacement. The mounting hardware looked grubby and old, but that, too, was camouflage. The fittings were new and came apart easily.

The "phone" flashed red again. The fourth download had failed, even more quickly than the previous three. She turned to glare at the display, but as she did, something tugged roughly at her sleeve, so she looked there, instead.

Just above her wrist, a hole had torn in the fabric. Someone had just shot at her.

"You've got company," Dixon announced. "There's a window cleaner rig on the south—"

"They *aren't* window cleaners," Sydney said. She ducked and rolled, throwing herself behind the sheltering hulk of the air conditioner cabinet, seeking cover. The flat whistle of suppressed pistol fire sounded. More slugs dug into the tar-and-gravel roofing, kicking up puffs of dust and dirt. Sydney slid one hand inside her coverall, reaching for her own weapon as she peered out from behind her cover.

At the far end of the expansive roof, two men had come up and over the edge. Now, a third followed. All wore drab coveralls, with billed hats pulled low over their faces. Each carried a pistol, field-finished matte black, and the three-man unit moved with easy coordination. This was undoubtedly a tactical team, practiced and professional.

She hadn't expected anything like this. No one had. The surveillance switch had been presented as drudge work. Opposition had seemed unlikely in the original assignment.

That didn't mean Sydney had come unprepared, though. Her pistol was special issue, a .32 caliber Beretta with a grip molded to her hand. The blunt Magnum bullets it fired had more stopping power than most of such small size, but they were unlikely to carry far and endanger bystanders. Sydney scarcely felt the gun's recoil as she squeezed the trigger twice. One of the three men staggered and fell back, then moved forward again.

Body armor. They were better outfitted for this kind of work than she was.

She pulled herself back behind the air conditioner unit. She moved just in time. More bullets punched into the surrounding rooftop. Sparks and metal shards flew as one round careened off of the cabinet itself. They had found her range. Sydney realized that her first impression was correct: These were professionals. She knew from experience how difficult it was to shoot accurately while on the move. These men seemed to have mastered the skill.

But moving targets were hard to hit too.

She shot again. This time, the bullet found her target's shoulder, beyond the protection of his body armor. The man yelped and stumbled, falling against one of his comrades. Instinctively, the others turned to look.

Sydney took advantage of their momentary distraction. She dove from her hiding place, throwing herself forward in a long, low leap that flowed neatly into a full-body roll. As she leaped, she snatched the surveillance unit free of its housing. Even as she bounced and rolled across the roof, she shoved the device into a coverall pocket.

"Halt!" one of the men yelled.

Sydney ignored the command. More pressing matters commanded her attention. Her unknown attackers were between her and the rooftop exit now. The gravel-strewn roof was rough beneath her fingertips as she pulled out of her roll and regained her feet. She began to run.

The gun was still in her hand, she suddenly realized. There was no real use she could make of it now, so she rammed it under her belt. Without breaking stride, she unzipped the top part of her coverall completely and groped for the harness that she was wearing underneath.

"Outrigger, I'm taking the emergency exit," she gasped into her comm-link. "Be out front."

"Roger, Phoenix," Dixon said, all business.

The muzzle-suppressed guns whistled again, three shots in quick succession. Sydney felt the rooftop vibrate as more bullets found it. Gravel shrapnel stung her calves. She zigzagged a bit, but never lost sight of her target, the dark opening of an airshaft. Below its lip was a pair of neatly intersecting cross-braces. She took a deep breath as the opening came closer.

This was going to hurt.

"Halt!" the man ordered again.

One last footstep took her over the shaft's edge. Her right hand drew the grappling hook from beneath her jumpsuit. In the single, transcendent instant as lateral motion was joined by vertical drop, she eyed the shaft's cross-braces. She angled her body like a diver and plunged between them. As the two metal beams passed though her field of view, she cast the hook. It caught and held.

Sydney fell into the gloom. The dirty brick shaft lining slid past her more and more rapidly, and air whistled in her ears. A whining sound came from her descent harness as cable unwound. Time seemed to slow as floors passed, one after another.

This was *really* going to hurt.

Bullets ricocheted from the airshaft walls. Her pursuers had reached the opening. Sydney kicked at one wall, then another, swinging back and forth to evade their shots. The world rocked crazily, but Sydney watched the airshaft walls continue to slide past, estimating the extent of her fall.

She drew her pistol again and pointed it upward. She squeezed off two shots without even looking up to aim, as much to divert as to defend. They were almost certain to follow her, and she had to do anything she could to delay that. Spent rounds might fall back and injure her, but she had to take the risk.

A pause in enemy fire rewarded the effort. They had pulled back, even if only for a moment. That was good. She put the pistol away again and clutched the harness's control grip instead.

The descent harness had enough cable for a full-distance drop, but the longer she fell, the harder it would be to stop. She braced herself and squeezed the grip.

The webbed straps of the harness she was wearing under her clothes dug into her muscular body. The cable went taut. Metal squealed as heavy springs coiled inside the cable reel wound tight and greedily drank the velocity of her drop.

Even with time to prepare, even with the harness absorbing so much of her momentum, Sydney felt as if the entire world had risen up and slapped her. The jolting halt drove the air from her lungs in an explosive burst and put spots before her eyes.

When her vision cleared, she hung in mid-air, deep in the airshaft's shadowed gloom. She sucked air desperately and surveyed her surroundings.

A louvered vent cover was within easy reach. She groped along its framework and dug into it with strong hands. She pulled. Metal groaned again, and then she had torn the cover completely free. She dropped it and then squirmed through the opening beyond. A moment later she twisted the harness cable disconnect and dropped to her feet to take the measure of her surroundings. She was in a cubicle farm. Countless nondescript people boxes filled a common area. The overhead lights were dim.

Even for what had been intended as such a routine mission, APO's briefing had been thorough. It was Saturday, late afternoon. That meant the building was closed for business, but floor alarms were off to allow for cleaning crews. Sydney half-ran, half-walked through the shadowed workstations with pistol drawn and half-crouching for cover. She had to reach the exit before her pursuers found her.

"Hey! Who're *you*!?" The voice ahead was a woman's, startled and half-angry. Its source leaned out now from behind a cube partition. She was black and attractive, right on the edge between young and middle-aged, wearing casual clothes. "No one's supposed to be in here!"

Sydney had nearly said the same thing. Instead, she bit back the words and dropped into character. "Maintenance, ma'am." She gestured at the logo on her coverall. While that hand drew the woman's attention, the other moved to conceal the gun it held. "Vent system. Just checking. There've been some complaints." Her mind raced as she considered her options.

"Well, good lord, lady, of course there's been complaints!" The woman stood. She was taller than Sydney by two inches and towered over the cube's walls. Behind the woman, Sydney could now see a live computer and a clutter of paperwork. "During the week, this place is a real—"

The black woman's words stopped. Her expressive eyes rolled back, and then closed. A red blossom bloomed on her upper arm, and she slumped against a cubicle wall.

Sydney spun. Even before she had turned completely, her pistol was raised and half-aimed. It took her less than a second to nail the ersatz windowwasher who had followed her. This time, for whatever reason, her target fell down and stayed down.

More were sure to follow.

"What the hell?" the other woman mumbled. Her skin had taken on an ashen quality. She was in shock.

Driven by adrenaline and acting on instinct, Sydney helped the woman back into her seat and gave her injury a cursory inspection. It wasn't serious, as such things went. Still moving on autopilot,

Sydney rolled the chair and the woman it held into a nearby office. Sydney turned off the light and shut the door. The bystander would be safer there, but needed medical aid.

Unfortunately, getting help to her wasn't the only thing that needed to be done.

Sydney raced for the suite's door and through it into the hallway beyond. Twenty rapid steps took her to the floor's elevator lobby. There was no time to wait and no time to reach the stairs. She took the appropriate tool wrench from her kit and popped the metal doors open. The ozone scent of electrical motors drifted up from the darkness beyond. The elevator cage was two floors below. Sydney gripped the doorframe and leaned forward.

Two more rounds of silenced small-arms fire slammed into the elevator's doorframe, inches from her fingers.

Sydney jumped. This time, there was no descent harness to absorb her momentum, but the need was nowhere near as great. She made a perfect landing on the elevator roof and reached for the trapdoor. Pulling it free, she looked up just in time to see a figure framed in the open doorway above. It was another of her pursuers.

The trapdoor cover was bulky but light. She spun and sailed it upward, and was rewarded with a cry of pain as the square panel found its target. The man on the floor above fell back, stunned.

Sydney dropped into the passenger car and stabbed the button for the lobby. As the elevator traveled to the final floor, she glanced at her reflection in the polished metal control panel. Sydney was Chicana today, with black, straight hair and coppery skin. Just now, the hair was mussed. She tidied it a bit and adjusted her uniform. She could still feel the adrenaline rush but worked against it, forcing herself to breathe more slowly.

When the doors slid open at lobby level, she flawlessly assumed the role of maintenance technician again. It was a skill that had saved Sydney's life more times than marksmanship and hand-to-hand combat combined. When she had to, she could become someone else.

The guard at the front desk was the same fat man who had granted her access earlier. Then, he had given a long and appreciative gaze. Now, he paid more attention to his comic book as Sydney stepped out of the elevator.

"I need to go out to my truck," she said. She

waved the surveillance unit at him. "Thermocouple is fried."

The fat man grunted. "Just get it fixed," he said.

Sydney nodded. "We do what we can," she said, and headed for the front doors with utter nonchalance. Beyond them, she could see the waiting panel van. Dixon was behind the wheel, doing his best to look patient.

"We need to go," Sydney said as she slid into the seat beside him. "Fast. There was trouble."

"You're okay?" Dixon asked as he guided the vehicle back into traffic.

"Sore. Bungee jumping was never my sport," she said. There was a cell phone in the glove compartment. She grabbed it and entered 9-1-1. Dixon eyed her, but said nothing.

"Hello, yes?" Sydney's voice took on a tremulous falsetto and a slight Southern accent. "We need help here! Someone is shooting, and my friend is hurt. Oh my goodness, it looks bad." She continued for a moment with the same assumed voice, providing the dispatcher with the address and office number. She broke the connection when he asked her who she was.

"What was that all about?" Dixon asked. He sounded concerned, but kept his eyes on the busy street, driving aggressively to put distance between them and the job site.

"Collateral damage," Sydney said. "A civilian got hurt."

"The offices were supposed to be closed," Dixon said.

"We're not the only ones willing to work on Saturday," Sydney replied, sounding half-disgusted and half-guilty. She thought about the woman's yelp of pain and sudden collapse, and shook her head. "It shouldn't have happened."

"A lot of things happen that shouldn't," Dixon said. "That's part of the reason we have our jobs." He turned onto Constitution Avenue, the nation's Main Street, and headed for the Fourteenth Street Bridge. In minutes, they would be at Ronald Reagan National Airport. Already, sirens could be heard in the distance. "How bad was it?" he asked.

"Bad enough," Sydney said. She looked glumly at the small surveillance unit that she had retrieved from its rooftop installation. "Sloane won't be happy."

LOS ANGELES

"I am not happy," Arvin Sloane said. He sat at the head of the conference table in the brightly lit room. His weathered features were calm, even tranquil. One hand rested on the tabletop while the other stroked his chin. With his relaxed composure and lean, casual elegance he could have been posing for a portrait. Only a slight glint in his eyes evidenced the extent of his irritation as he gazed, in turn, at Sydney and Dixon, then at the other members of APO who were in attendance.

Dealing with Sloane was like gazing into a

spring-fed pond, Sydney had often thought. The surface was calm and the depths looked tranquil, but that tranquility was an illusion. Beneath the surface, treacherous currents held sway, invisible and unpredictable. They moved according to their own rules and could capture and destroy with casual ease, and knowing that those currents were there did not protect against them.

Jack Bristow, seated to Sloane's right, was no easier to read, but for different reasons. In recent years, Sydney had come to know that the mysteries in her father's depths were as turbulent as those within Sloane. The difference was that Sloane at least projected the illusion of openness. The facade of order and reserve that Jack Bristow showed the world was sometimes too obviously a mask.

Arvin Sloane nearly always seemed at peace and at ease. No one could ever say that about Jack Bristow. Anger, however well reined in and controlled, seemed to be his constant companion.

"We retrieved the unit," Sydney pointed out. She had delivered a written report upon returning from Washington and presented a verbal one to the gathered team. She was getting tired of discussing the assignment. "Per instructions."

"Retrieval was a fallback objective," Sloane said. "The primary objective, to correct the technical difficulties, was not achieved. The mission was a failure."

"The mission was a qualified success," Jack said.

Sloane actually smiled faintly at that. His lips curved in some microscopic percentage of an arc and then relaxed again, and he sighed. "In this instance, Jack," he said, "our measures of success are not quite the same."

The exchange was business as usual for Marcus Dixon and Michael Vaughn, seated on either side of Sydney. They had seen Sloane and Jack disagree, with at least apparent politeness, countless times before. Neither showed any particular response to the exchange. Nadia Santos, on the other side of the table, glanced from Sloane to Jack and back again, but said nothing. This was still new to her, and her features showed, if not worry, at least attentive concern.

Only Marshall Flinkman, seated next to Nadia, showed any particular agitation, but, then, Marshall always seemed slightly agitated. His dark, expressive eyes darted from side to side. His notebook computer was open before him, and he glanced at the screen, then at Sloane, then at Jack, and then at the computer again. His fingers drummed the tabletop silently, keeping time with some tune that only Marshall could hear. His seemed to be the only real energy at the table.

"Yes," Sloane said. "Sydney succeeded in retrieving the surveillance equipment with minimal damage." He paused. "And without significant incident," he continued.

Sydney felt her eyes narrow slightly and her lips purse, as if of their own volition. She thought about the flat squeak of suppressed pistol fire and about the men who had pursued her into the depths of the office building before she had lost them and escaped. She thought about the startled expression on the black woman's face and her yelp of pain as a bullet struck her.

"We didn't anticipate that kind of opposition," she said, more sharply than she intended. "No one did."

"A qualified success," Jack said again. His stolid pragmatism was a warning. "Very welcome, considering the expedited circumstances and what we found."

"What we found?" Sydney said. "I was told that this was a technical run. Were we looking for something?"

The mission had been a sudden one that afforded very little time to prepare. Vaughn's wireless call had pulled Sydney out of a charming patisserie less than an hour before launch. She and Dixon had been given only maps, diagrams, schedules, and tools, and the instructions on how to use them. They had been given the what, when, and where, but little in the way of why.

She and Dixon had been the "who," of course.

If he resented the question, the resentment didn't show. "Michael? If you will?" Sloane said.

Vaughn held a wireless computer mouse in one hand. He clicked it, once. On the conference room's big display screen appeared a greatly simplified map of Washington, D.C., and surrounding environs.

"It should come as no surprise to anyone here that the United States and the CIA have a vested interest in monitoring the activities of the former component states of the USSR," Vaughn said dryly.

No one laughed.

He clicked the mouse again. A red star appeared on the map. "Here is where our friends the Russians are known to maintain a front," Vaughn continued.

Sydney half-smiled as Marshall muttered, "I knew that," and Jack Bristow shrugged. This was pretty basic stuff, after all.

"For some years now, the Agency has maintained clandestine monitoring assets directed at this site. You might remember the scandal when some of those assets were discovered back in the 1980s." Vaughn clicked the mouse again and a second star appeared, in the section of the map devoted to downtown Washington, D.C. "To lessen the chance of another scandal, and as technological capabilities have improved, the Agency has been able to establish listening posts at greater remove from their target. One of these is—*was*—here." He nodded in Sydney's direction. "The location offers a number of other advantages, but what mattered was line-of-sight."

"This is all pretty basic," Nadia said, echoing Sydney's earlier thought.

Vaughn nodded again. "Background helps, though," he said. "Four days ago, our listening post experienced sudden and sharp signal degradation." He glanced to Nadia's left. "Marshall?"

Marshall, startled, looked up from whatever he had been considering on his computer screen. He took a deep breath and stood. The changes his life had seen in recent years, the marriage and the child, had done him good. More centered and poised than he had been in the days of SD-6, he still retained the boyish quality that Sydney had always found charming.

"These things are nothing special," he said, holding up one hand and pointing at it with the other. "Very reliable, field proven."

Everyone stared at him. His hand was empty.

Marshall blushed. "Uh," he said. He reached into a jacket pocket and withdrew the surveillance module that Sydney had retrieved. "These things are nothing special," he said, again, starting over. "Very reliable, field proven. This is a standard multimode, integrated surveillance unit, pretty much standard-issue these days but still very nice. I helped work out some of the software protocols last year, back when we were all—well, most of us, anyway—in Langley. They always work, except when they don't."

He sat again, clearly pleased to have been the center of attention, however briefly.

"And when they don't, Langley gets concerned. That was four days ago," Vaughn said. "Luckily we had appropriate, untasked assets available."

Three days ago, Sydney had been enjoying some hard-earned leave. She had been nibbling pâté and truffles in Georgetown when the call had come. Presumably, Dixon's call had come earlier.

"'Untasked' as in 'on leave,'" Sydney said. "I don't understand the urgency. Equipment repair isn't even the kind of work we usually do."

"Usually." The word drifted up from Sloane like cigarette smoke, lazy and slow. "And that should be *attempted* equipment repair."

"Background helps," Vaughn said again. "The reason we moved so quickly is that for the past three months, at least, the CIA monitors have been tracking back-channel chatter involving K-Directorate and a major black-market arms shipment."

K-Directorate was, more or less, a modern equivalent of the old KGB, the USSR's intelligence and espionage arm. It was at once that agency's predecessor and successor, yet another segment of the old Soviet bureaucracy that had survived into the post–Cold War world.

"K is selling weapons in the United States?"

Nadia asked, plainly surprised. It didn't track with the enemy agency's typical operations.

"Not selling. Buying, perhaps, or coordinating the sale. Or monitoring. We really don't know," Vaughn said.

"We do know that they've taken an active interest," Sloane said. "And we do know that it's something sizable." He fixed Sydney with a steady gaze. "Which explains the urgency of the surveillance effort."

"You're right, Vaughn," Sydney said. "Background helps."

Vaughn said nothing, but gestured at Marshall. This time, the technical expert was ready to take the floor. He held up the retrieved surveillance unit again. "Like I said," he said, "these are very reliable. But they're not easy to place and align. Our intent was to leave the unit in place and replace the internal operating system. Software, it's like power. It corrupts." He paused, waiting for laughter, only to look vaguely disappointed when it didn't come.

Sydney recalled the modified cell phone she had used on the rooftop, and the flashing red light of its display as each download failed. "Reloading didn't work," she said.

"That's right," Marshall agreed. "And here's why." Though still somewhat clumsy in social situations and given to nervous twitches, he had remarkably skilled hands. He twisted the unit's housing and used a pair of insulated forceps to extract a module the size of a shirt button. "This isn't ours," he said. "Well, it's ours *now,* spoils of war and all that, but—"

"Specifics, please," Sloane prodded. Marshall's technical expertise bought him considerable patience and accommodation, but there were limits.

"Okay, okay," Marshall said. He pointed at the original unit, and then at the smaller component, saying, "This is nice. This is even nicer. It's a piggyback monitor chip, a store-and-forward incremental tap that copied our feed. It's got a microburst gamma-ray satellite relay in it that dumps the buffer every 17.6 hours. Five days ago an interface glitch cropped up and impacted our own signal. If that hadn't happened, we might never have found it."

"Whose satellite assets have a 17.6-hour periodicity?" Dixon asked. "Alone or in combination?"

"Don't know yet," Marshall said. They were words that he almost never said, especially in the technical arena. "No single entity's, that's for sure. But I'm running a regression algorithm—"

"We're trying to determine whose tap it is," Sloane interjected. "But I think it's safe that we'll need to deal with them. They clearly aren't on the side of the angels."

Again, Sydney's mind's eye filled with the image of men in window-washer uniforms. This time, she did not even begin to speak. Disgust stilled her tongue.

"Have you been able to determine how long it had been in place?" Sloane asked.

Marshall nodded eagerly. "At least two months," he said. "Chemical analysis of the bonding agents used says—"

"Thank you, Marshall," Sloane said before Marshall could launch into a longer explanation.

Marshall dropped back into his seat. He seemed half-pleased and half-sad that his time in the spotlight had come to an end.

Sloane continued. "Jack?"

"I appreciate that the last operation was with little notice," the elder Bristow said. His words were clipped and businesslike, spoken in the same pragmatic tones that he might use to order lunch, or to direct someone's execution. "Consider this fair warning. The next operation will be on short notice too." He paused and pointed. "Sydney, Marcus, and Vaughn especially should keep yourselves available. Be ready to move fast."

Everyone nodded.

Jack bulldozed on. "Marshall, you're on call too. Work with Weiss to backtrack the tap, and get with me to discuss outfitting. Nadia can be your backup on this." He paused and glanced at Sloane, yielding the floor.

"Before we adjourn, I'd like to say something," Sloane said. "I mentioned earlier that this was a qualified success. I need to stress that my concern had nothing to do with any personal shortcomings in performance."

Sydney glanced at Dixon, then Vaughn. Both shrugged, however slightly, and she shrugged back. Sloane's comments were an across-the-board surprise.

"We live in perilous times, people," the APO chief continued. "And that peril has made Washington a very difficult place to do our kind of business. The security checkpoints and closed streets make local missions more difficult, and render conventional emergency extractions very difficult."

"We made it through all right," Sydney replied, sharply.

Sloane continued. "The same measures that are intended to protect civilians can put them in greater danger. I'd like all of you to be cognizant of that in the future." He took a breath. "If nothing else, collateral damage ensures bad publicity and threatens security."

No one said anything to that.

"Until later, then," Sloane said in dismissal. As chairs slid back and attendees stood to leave, he continued. "Sydney?" he said. "A moment, please."

She remained seated as the others left, perfectly happy to keep most of the table between them. She hated being alone with him. She hated the earnest look of near-parental concern in his eyes as he spoke to her. She hated his voice, cool and dark and liquid, like the smoke that beekeepers used to befuddle their charges.

"What happened yesterday wasn't due to any failing on your part," Sloane said.

"I know that," she responded, not entirely sincerely. "But the idea that we were there just to tidy up—"

"It was important," Sloane said. "And Marshall's discovery suggests that it's more important than we thought."

She said nothing.

"About the civilian—" Sloane started.

"The civilian?" Sydney said sharply.

"I assumed you knew, even if it hasn't made the news media," he said. He favored her with one of his rare expressions of surprise, however mild. It was so unexpected that she suspected it was deliberate. "I had Weiss research the matter. A minor wound, in and out, no major damage."

"How bad?" she demanded. Experience had taught her to never trust his first response to any question.

"Get with Weiss about it," Sloane said. "He has the details. He's busy backtracking your escape, scrubbing surveillance cameras and the like."

"Why are you telling me this?" she nearly hissed.

Sloane looked at her levelly. "You're a study in contradictions, Sydney. You're one of the best operatives I've ever worked with or against."

"I'm not sure that's a compliment," she said.

"Be that as it may, one of the factors that

makes you so good is your passion—and your com-passion. But they can be weaknesses, as well."

Again, there seemed to be no reply that she could make. Sloane was in full paternalistic mode now. His words and tone made her skin crawl. She had enough difficulties with one father. She didn't need another, let alone one with Sloane's history.

It was if he had read her mind. The smile on his tired features now was a rueful one. "I know that some of the things I've had to do have dam-aged our relationship terribly, Sydney," he said. "And I'm sorry for that. I'd be even sorrier if you thought I was trying to remake you in my image, in any way. What happened yesterday was an acci-dent, and would not have happened at all but for the urgency of our timetable."

She almost believed him.

"Syd. Hey." Vaughn gestured as she left the meet-ing room. "Over here."

"Over here" was APO operative Eric Weiss's workstation. Vaughn was hovering there, and Sydney had the distinct impression that she had been invited to interrupt a session of Guy Talk. That was fine with her.

She smiled up at Vaughn without comment, and then down at the seated Weiss. "Hi, Eric. I was coming to see you, anyway."

Weiss grunted in acknowledgment. He was one of the few men whom Sydney had ever met who could do that amiably. Without taking his eyes from his computer screen, he responded, "How'd the big confab go? Any fireworks?"

"We missed you," was Sydney's only response. Vaughn had no doubt told him anything he needed to know already. "How's the backtrack work going?"

"Almost done," Eric said. His fingertips danced across the keyboard. "What I can do is almost done, that is. When you detoured into the building, you passed some security cameras that we hadn't prepped, you know." He looked up briefly and glanced at her.

Sydney shrugged. "I knew that I might," she said. "I didn't have much choice."

"Well, the disguise should take care of those. I can't do much about them, anyway. But to be on the safe side, Sloane's got me hacking into the local banks and such, deleting or corrupting the feed from incidental security cameras." He sighed. "You would not *believe* how many ATMs there are in that block. You and Dixon look to have passed in front of each and every one."

That was an exaggeration, Sydney knew, but there was no point in arguing it. "Sloane said—"

Eric stopped typing. He spun in his chair. "He said you'd want this," he said, and passed her a document folder. It was generic manila, not color-coded for any security level. Ten or so pages of closely set type and photographic images waited within.

"What is it, Syd?" Vaughn asked. He had been quiet as she spoke with Weiss, but she had felt his attentive gaze on her throughout the conversation.

"Background," Sydney said, and began to read.

"Hospital medical records," Weiss said to Vaughn, correcting her.

Among the most basic of Sydney's skills was her ability to read rapidly and comprehensively. She scanned the computer printouts while the two men reverted to Guy Talk mode. By the time Vaughn had explained why the Washington Redskins were a better football team than the Dallas Cowboys and Eric Weiss had responded that he was insane, she had finished the dossier.

The name of the woman in the office building was Keisha Wyatt. Sydney examined her photo for a long moment. It looked familiar, and not just from the incident. Keisha was thirty-eight but looked younger. She had excellent health coverage through her employer and a bullet hole in her upper left arm. The incoming slug had shattered the humerus, and a bone splinter had nicked an artery. In all, it was messier than Sloane had indicated, but Wyatt's doctors' records showed that medical attention had come in time and that a full recovery was anticipated.

"Everything okay?" Vaughn asked as she closed the folder and handed it to Weiss, who promptly fed its contents into a shredder.

"Not as okay as I would like," Sydney said honestly. "I feel terrible about that poor woman."

"She's going to recover," Weiss said.

"She shouldn't *need* to recover," Sydney said, more sharply than she had intended. She didn't like seeing civilians hurt.

Neither man said anything for a long moment, until Vaughn broke the awkward silence. "You didn't know," he said. "You couldn't know. The offices were closed. You did everything you could to protect her, and everything you could to get help."

"It shouldn't have happened," Sydney said doggedly.

"We had to move fast, Sydney," Vaughn said.

"I still don't understand that. Equipment repair isn't the kind of thing we usually do," Sydney said. "I mean, a job is a job, but—"

Vaughn gestured, interrupting her. "Think about what Marshall told us," he said. "The 'button' downloaded every 17.6 hours, and it had been in place for a while. It acted up five days ago. Why?"

"Marshall seemed to think it was chance," Sydney said.

Vaughn did not so much dismiss the explanation so much as he ignored it. He continued: "And why was an armed response team in the area and so ready to come after you?"

CHAPTER 3

LOS ANGELES

"Shopping was more fun as a civilian," Nadia said as she and Sydney wended their way between mannequins and attendants. Denize's Armoire, high on Rodeo Drive, was their fifth shop of the day, and new to Sydney's experience. In fact, it was new, period, and Sydney had to wonder how long the place would last.

The place was a contradictory mix of the trendy and retro. Elegant ensembles on display combined bright fabrics draped in form-flattering lines, accentuated by industrial-look accessories. The outfit that had caught Nadia's eye was of tightly woven scarlet material. It looked like it had been draped loosely on a willowy plastic form, then closed and given shape by a series of silver clasps that evoked classic industrial design elements. Sydney thought it looked absolutely ghastly, but refrained from saying so. Instead, she asked, "What do you mean?"

"So much of the work is fantasy, imagination, even role-playing. I have always thought that trying on a new outfit is like auditioning for a play, or a new role," Nadia said. "But the clothes we wear on the job, the places we go and the things we do—"

"Hmmm," Sydney said. She nodded. "I see what you mean." She watched as Nadia stroked the perfectly draped fabric and then pinched it gently. "This is very nice material," she said.

"A new arrival," the shop's owner said, suddenly at Nadia's side. She was an attractive woman in her late middle ages, well-preserved and poised, and the fact that she wore no nametag made it likely that this was the eponymous Denize. Her hand moved quickly and plucked Nadia's from the displayed dress. "Very nice, and very dear," she said. "Very, very dear."

Sydney was vaguely surprised that the woman had been able to approach two experienced espionage agents undetected, much less touch one with such presumption, but she supposed that salespeople had their methods. Besides, Denize had the advantage of working in familiar territory.

Nadia seemed unfazed by the implication that she was in some way unworthy of the shop's wares. She smiled slightly. "This is Espinoza's work, I think?" she asked, gesturing at the garish dress.

The expertise came as a surprise both to Sydney and to the shop's owner. "Yes," Denize said, with new unctuousness. She focused on Nadia now, to the near-exclusion of her half sister. Her nostrils actually flared a bit, as if at the scent of money. "You're familiar with Espinoza? We're his exclusive distributor in the United States. These are all designer originals."

"He works with limited-edition blends," Nadia said to Sydney with calm authority. "Alpaca, linen, silk—all dyed in the thread. Very limited."

"Each ensemble is a piece of art," the shop owner purred, anxious to curry favor and make the sale. "This one would look wonderful on you. With your proportions—"

Nadia made the kind of smile that really wasn't a smile at all. "It looked wonderful on me in Barcelona," she said. "Last year."

The older woman blinked, startled. "I—that's not possible," she said, and gestured at the neighboring mannequins, all adorned with what looked to be Espinoza designs. Some of them looked nearly wearable. "These are new for this year, all of them. I assure you."

"Thank you for speaking with us," Nadia said in dismissal. Her voice was so cool that icicles seemed to descend from each word. Denize gasped, then turned away from them.

It was only a minute later, outside, in the warm Beverly Hills sun, that Sydney allowed herself to laugh. Nadia laughed, too, adjusted the smoked lenses she wore, and smiled. "She may be more polite next time," Nadia said.

"May," Sydney half-agreed. She had shopped Rodeo before. The various logos that decorated the bags she and Nadia were carrying were old acquaintances. Versace, Ralph Lauren, YSL, and their friends had joined forces to leave their marks on her credit record. "But I think that it's part of the job to condescend."

Nadia gave a delicate, ladylike snort. "Shop-people," she said.

The sidewalks flanking Rodeo Drive were as crowded as usual. Sydney was intensely aware of appreciative gazes as they made their way along the bustling thoroughfare. She knew from personal experience that Los Angeles's population included a larger percentage of attractive women than nearly any city on Earth. Sometimes it seemed that more of that complement worked harder to be seen than their equivalents just about anywhere else. Even so, Nadia and Sydney stood out. More than a few men smiled at them, and more than a few tried to lock eyes.

"Where to now?" Nadia asked. Numerous other shops were within easy walking distance, each as exclusive and as snootily staffed as the one they had just left. "We have not completely mortgaged our futures yet, I think."

"We should get something to eat," Sydney said. Her hands were full, so she nodded to her left. Beyond a barrier of delicate-looking rails awaited an oasis of small tables and chairs. A moment later, she and her half sister were among the sidewalk café's patrons, under the shading canopy.

"Why do it, then?" Sydney asked without

preamble. When Nadia looked up quizzically from the menu, she continued. "Why shop, if it's not fun?"

Nadia laughed. "I did not say it wasn't fun anymore," she said. "I said that it is not as *much* fun."

They spoke softly. It was prudent to avoid sensitive topics or espionage-specific names and terminology. Sydney was reasonably confident that the subdued chatter of their fellow patrons would make eavesdropping difficult, but discretion was always a good idea.

"Maybe not at first," Sydney said. For all her worldliness, Nadia was still relatively new to the game. "Your perspective is different at first. You look at everything with new eyes. But you get used to the work, and life goes on." She smiled. "It goes on, but it gets crazy sometimes."

Nadia laughed, then looked up again as their waiter approached.

"Ladies," he said, with brisk, professional good cheer. He set glasses of cracked ice before them and poured from a pitcher of water. "So nice to see you both. Would you like to know our specials?" When Nadia nodded, be began a list of light lunch entrées with heavy prices.

Idly, Sydney wondered if he had another life

too. The likelihood that an espionage agent—of any agency—would be working at an L.A. café was unlikely, but other possibilities remained. He had pretty-boy good looks and a trained voice, and the way he moved demonstrated a ready, constant awareness of his body language. On a whim, she interrupted.

"Excuse me," she asked, feeling suddenly playful. "Have I seen you somewhere?"

He paused, and grinned. This time, he looked entirely sincere.

Sydney continued. It was a guess, but a safe one, given where they were. "On television, perhaps?"

"An aspirin commercial," he said, clearly flattered that she seemed to have recognized him. "I'm the annoying coworker."

"I *knew* you looked familiar!" Sydney lied. The city was full of aspiring actors, busing tables even as they looked for lives of glamour. She pointed at him and looked in her sister's direction. "This is the guy from that aspirin commercial!" she said. "The annoying coworker!"

Nadia, to her great credit, caught the conversational ball and ran with it. "Really!" she said. "Service by a celebrity!"

The waiter was nearly ecstatic now. "Oh, I know you josh," he said. "But you've really made my day! I can't wait to tell my roommate. This is better than any tip!"

He was still beaming a moment later when he finished taking their orders. He was moving with new energy and grace.

"That was kind of you," Nadia said. "But a lie." She hadn't been fooled.

"I like to people-watch," Sydney said. "And guesses like that make for good practice." She sipped cool water. "The job has a lot of improvisation to it."

Nadia nodded. "I know that," she responded, not defensively but with casual confidence.

"I know it too," Sydney said. "But I relearn it every assignment."

The waiter, still beaming, returned with their drinks, a pair of Kirs. They were glasses of white wine, each with a splash of crème de cassis. Both women raised them, and each waited for the other to propose a toast. After a long second, Sydney filled the silence. "To sisters," she said. "And housemates."

"To sisters," Nadia echoed. After the two glasses had clicked together, she continued. "And is that what today is about? Not just about shopping."

The Kir was cool and refreshing, a good choice for a warm summer day. Sydney savored the first taste before responding. "I thought we should have fun," she said. "We work together. We're living together. Shopping seemed like the logical next step."

Nadia laughed. "It's a good thought," she said.

"So was your comment, back at the shop," Sydney said. She thought back to Nadia's disdain for the red dress, and gazed off into the distance for a moment. "It *was* more fun as a civilian."

So often reserved and even dignified, Nadia abruptly looked impish. "It's *always* fun to spend money," she said.

Their orders arrived. Light salads of tomato and mozzarella lay on beds of crisp, salted zucchini strips. Sydney's included smoked salmon, sliced as fine as angel-hair pasta, but Nadia had opted for chicken instead. The waiter hovered for a moment, still pleased by Sydney's casual bit of improvisation, but soon they were alone again.

"This is good," Nadia said between bites.

"French, I think," Sydney said. "At least, except for the salmon. Did you know that French cooking is what's served at all United States state dinners? We don't have our own haute cuisine."

"The current political climate makes that an interesting choice," Nadia said drily.

Sydney shrugged. "I don't think anyone selected French deliberately," she said.

"But the choice was made." Nadia ate faster than she drank. Her lunch salad had half-disappeared, but fully three quarters of her Kir remained.

"So," Sydney said. "We've spent money, you've broken poor Denize's spirit, I've made our waiter's day, and we've eaten trendy salads. What else do single gals do with their days?"

"Talk about boyfriends," Nadia responded almost instantly. "You and Michael."

"'Boyfriend'?" Sydney said. She arched a brow quizzically.

Nadia laughed. "Lover. Significant other. Whichever term you wish to use."

Sydney wondered about that for a moment. "I—I don't know," she finally said. "The past few years have been—difficult."

Even the delicate phrasing churned painful memories. Her entire life had been turned on its head more than once. The complex game of deep-cover espionage had claimed so many she had known and loved. Friends, family, and lovers had died, in some part because of who Sydney was and what she did. Two years of her own life had been taken from her. The most nightmarish part of it all was the fate of her mother, who had been presumed dead since Sydney's childhood. But Irina Derevko had resurfaced, alive and well and herself a part of the endless game. Derevko, mother to both Sydney and Nadia, had been executed on orders from Jack Bristow, acting to save Sydney's life.

Her own mother had taken out a contract on Sydney's life. Sydney's father had eliminated her, to protect Sydney. Even now that she knew the truth of the situation, Sydney could scarcely believe it.

Through much of it, Vaughn had been a comfort and a reservoir of strength. It was Vaughn who had facilitated her transition from the rogue cell that was SD-6 to CIA proper. It had been Vaughn who had been her primary contact during the months she'd worked to bring down SD-6, and Vaughn who had been her close coworker the months that followed. It had been Vaughn who had given her the love and support she had so desperately needed. He had been the one constant in her life.

And it was Vaughn who, during Sydney's two years of missing-and-presumed-dead status, had found someone new and married her. That the woman had proven to be a double agent didn't make things any better.

Sydney blinked, setting the memories aside. She was back in the restaurant, with Nadia seated across from her and nibbling on a slice of radish.

"Life goes on," Nadia said. The other woman's expressive dark eyes were unblinking and calm. She spoke with an easy pragmatism.

"It does," Sydney said. She envied Nadia's demeanor sometimes. Her half sister knew much of Sydney's background, but not all of it. She certainly had not experienced the complex emotional crosscurrents that made pursuit of a relationship difficult. "And very fast. There's so much to do. And the new arrangements take some getting used to."

"You've worked with everyone before," Nadia prodded.

Sydney nodded. "And some of them, I'd rather never work with again."

"My father," Nadia said. It wasn't a question.

"I'm sorry," Sydney said, but her regret was less for her words than for the situation she had found herself in. She worked once more under the direction of someone she hated, and worked closely with that man's daughter.

She continued. "Vaughn is single again, but that's a pretty recent development. He's got a lot of baggage, and God knows, I do. We're taking it slow for now."

"What about Weiss?" Nadia asked. Her radish was gone now, so she attacked a baby carrot. Her fine white teeth shredded it rapidly.

"What about him?" Sydney asked. She pushed her now-empty plate aside.

"Have you and he ever . . ." Nadia's words trailed off.

"No," Sydney half-said, half-laughed. "He's a wonderful guy, but not the boy for me."

"He's interesting," Nadia said. The two words were precisely the kind of noncommittal observation that Sydney had heard Nadia make many times before. They left an impression somewhere between aloof and mysterious.

"He is," Sydney said, not sure what she was agreeing with. She had seen the signals exchanged between Nadia and the other APO operative. She sipped her drink.

"I hope things work better for you and Michael," Nadia said, suddenly earnest. "I like adventure, I like excitement, but stability is good too."

"Well, thank you," Sydney said. "That's one reason I try so hard to maintain a home life."

Nadia nodded. "A foundation," she said.

Even with all the attendant issues that were sure to ensue, Sydney was glad that she had invited Nadia to be her housemate. She genuinely liked the other woman and enjoyed her company. "I like having a place to come back to. And I'm glad you're part of that place."

Nadia smiled, giving warmth to her typically reserved features. "It must be easier, now that I'm in the business."

Her point was good, if painful. Sydney's tumultuous life had taken a toll, but that toll had been even greater for those she knew and loved. Poor, sweet Danny Hecht, her fiancé, had been killed and her friend, Will Tippen, had seen his career in journalism destroyed—both in the name of secrecy. And so many others had died at the hands of enemies.

"Rooming with a civilian didn't work out very well," she said slowly, a catch in her voice.

"Francie?" Nadia asked.

"Francie," Sydney agreed sadly.

The late Francine Calfo had been Sydney's friend since college days. As graduate students, they had shared a home. It had been an especially attractive arrangement for Francie. She had enjoyed roomy, comfortable spaces while her good friend and largely absentee housemate pursued her studies and, supposedly, worked for the Credit Dauphine bank. Francie had never learned the secret of Sydney's double life. Even so, an adversary from that life had risen up and destroyed her. Worse, Francie had been replaced with a precise duplicate, who had later perished at Sydney's hand.

In a very real sense, Francie had died twice.

"You miss her, don't you?" Nadia asked, probing gently. Sydney had told her about Francie when she moved in, but they had never talked about her in great detail.

"I—I really don't think much about her anymore," Sydney said, surprising herself. "It's been more than two years, really, and work has kept me pretty busy, to put it lightly." She paused. "But yes, I miss her. We were good friends—sisters, almost." She paused again. "I never really had a chance to say good-bye. I don't even think there was a proper funeral."

The sunny restaurant seemed a bit less bright now, and Sydney's meal had lost its attraction. She pushed the remaining food around on her plate, toying with it so that she could avoid meeting Nadia's gaze.

It was difficult talking about someone who had died to someone who had somewhat taken her place.

Nadia cleared her throat. "Let's talk about something else, then," she said. She smiled. "Tell me more about Eric."

The ball was coming at him fast and low. Michael Vaughn dove forward and swung his right hand upward, using his momentum to boost the parry. When hand and ball met, they met hard. The ball went spinning away, to pound into the handball court wall. It bounced off with a solid, meaty sound that echoed in the enclosed space.

Eric Weiss made a sound between a yelp and a gasp as he intercepted the ball on first rebound. As the black sphere spun away, he dropped back to widen his field of play. He sucked air and said, "So, what's with you and Sydney?"

"Cut it out," Vaughn said, hitting the ball again. Weiss had tried gambits like this before, asking questions in an attempt to break his concentration. He was used to it, but he didn't like it. "No distractions."

This time, the ball ricocheted from the wall at a sharp angle and hit the floor. Weiss had to jump up nearly a foot to make the intercept and even then, his swing barely connected. The ball hit the front court wall and then the back, its trajectory noticeably wobbling. Vaughn retuned it easily and with even greater force.

"Gah!" Weiss said. Despite his occasional clowning, he was a good player, if not quite as good as Vaughn. He hit the ball hard, launching it into a nice three-point carom. Lightning fast, the black orb struck the front wall, then floor, then right wall, and then raced for the back wall along a downward vector. Barely in time, Vaughn slapped the ball to the wall again. This time, Weiss missed and the ball struck the floor twice.

Vaughn shook his head as he scooped up the ball in one gloved hand. "My serve," he said, and positioned himself in the service zone marked on the court floor.

"No, really, enquiring minds want to know," Weiss said. His voice echoed hollowly in the court's confines. "You and Syd. What's up?"

Sweat was running down Vaughn's face. With a sour expression he pushed back his eye protectors and wiped aside the beads of perspiration. He said nothing.

"She didn't like what Sloane had to say," Weiss said.

"She almost never does," Vaughn said. He tossed the ball straight up and caught it, then repeated the action. Eric was a good friend, but his observation was a reminder of just how relationships between the various members of APO were. For reasons that defied easy understanding, Arvin Sloane clearly took a paternal interest in Sydney, which added another layer of complexity. Human nature being what it was, Sydney sometimes responded to Sloane's directives like a contrary daughter.

"But at the debrief—"

"She was unhappy with the D.C. assignment," Vaughn said. He continued to loft the ball and catch it, letting his hand memorize its heft. "It was supposed to be routine scut work."

Weiss shrugged. "Given the way things went

down, better she on that rooftop than Marshall," he said.

That was true. In recent months, Marshall Flinkman's skills set had grown considerably. His personal life had finally bloomed, and he had begun to undertake field missions with some regularity. Even so, Vaughn doubted that Marshall would have been able to acquit himself as well as Sydney had when opposition arose.

Like a cracking whip, Vaughn's arm snapped back and then down. His wrist twisted, and his fingers opened. The handball slammed into the floor of the service zone, and Vaughn struck it when its rebound carried it to chest level. It was still moving very fast when it struck the court's front wall.

"Hey!" Weiss yelled, taken by surprise. The caroming ball was headed right at him. Reflexively, he dodged. Too late, he realized his mistake. Interception and effective return would have been possible if he had stayed where he was. Instead, the ball hit the floor again, two times in rapid succession, taking it out of play.

"That's not what I meant," Weiss continued. He seemed barely to notice the flubbed return. "I mean the wrist-slap."

Vaughn looked at him balefully. "Sydney's a big girl," he said.

Weiss continued. This time, his gaze remained locked on the ball in the other player's control. "I don't think she liked the private chat with Sloane, either," he said.

Vaughn shrugged. He watched Weiss watch him as he bounced the ball up and down leisurely. "Sydney feels things very deeply, Eric," he said. "Even after all she's been through, she hasn't built up a whole lot of emotional callousness."

"Not like you, huh?" Weiss asked.

The casual comment hurt. Vaughn's entire life had been marked by tragedy, beginning with the death in his childhood of his father. He had been a CIA operative and had died in the line of duty. Vaughn's initial relationship with Sydney had been interrupted by her two-year disappearance, and by his own marriage to a woman who had turned out to be a double agent. That marriage, in turn, had ended by his hand.

There was a time when Vaughn had thought he would spend the rest of his life with a newfound love. Instead, he had killed her and destroyed their home.

"Yeah," he said. "All callus, that's me."

Weiss didn't seem to realize that he had offended him. He was still watching Vaughn bounce the ball up and down. "Hey," he asked, "do we have a game here?"

On a final rebound, Vaughn put the ball back into play at last. He punched at it with sudden anger, catching it squarely with the flat surface of his gloved fist.

Anger had its cost. The ball rocketed toward the court wall at impressive speed, but along a sloppy trajectory. It hit, bounced, and then bounced again. Weiss intercepted it neatly, with a punishing swipe that made it carom from right-court wall and then the floor, and then to the left-court wall. Vaughn barely managed to catch it with his next swing.

"Close shave," Eric said, diving forward to intercept the ball again.

"Less talk," Vaughn said.

Another five minutes of hectic play passed as the match moved inexorably toward its conclusion. Vaughn forced his irritation to become something else, a mix of concentration and energy that accelerated his play. Again and again he sent the ball careening about the brightly lit confines of the handball court; again and again he leaped or dove just in time to counter Weiss's smashing returns. When an angled bounce sent the ball beyond his opponent's reach one final time, both men were panting for breath.

"Whoa," Weiss said. Sweat ran in rivers down his face and neck. He grabbed a towel from a sidelines rack and wiped himself dry. "Good match."

Vaughn nodded. "No one else needs the court," he said. "Want another match?"

"Hah. No, no, I don't think so," Weiss said. "Lose two, win one, that's enough." He paused. "Seriously, Mike, how are things with you and Sydney? You two have always been like chocolate and peanut butter, but not lately."

"A lot's happened lately," Vaughn said. At last, he let himself smile, but the expression was a wry one. "Sydney's been through a lot. So have I."

"Uh-huh," Weiss said, nodding. "But you're— you're single again, and you're working together. You're good together, Mike."

"I know, Eric," Vaughn said. "But we're taking it slow. So much has changed."

"But a lot has changed back," Weiss said. "We're all working together again. Even Sloane."

Vaughn, panting and tired and still wary of

Weiss's questions, managed a wry smile at that one. "How about you and Nadia, Eric? Any news on that front?"

Weiss shook his head. "Nothing," he said. "Nothing yet."

"Wouldn't that be strange, dating Arvin Sloane's daughter?" Vaughn asked.

Weiss laughed. "Isn't it strange sometimes, dating Jack Bristow's daughter?" he asked in return.

Jack Bristow's knuckles rapped on the open door. It was a courtesy knock only. He was already inside Arvin Sloane's office when he asked, "Arvin? A moment of your time?"

Sloane moved with cool efficiency as he blanked the screen on his computer and turned his chair to face his visitor. "Of course, Jack. I was just thinking about you."

Arvin Sloane's desktop was immaculate, and the little that it held was neatly arrayed. A pen-and-pencil set, a single legal pad perfectly aligned with the desktop edge, and a page-a-day calendar that could have been an illustration in an office supply catalog. There were no framed pictures, no paperweights, and no clutter of any sort. But for a mug of coffee and the coaster beneath it, there was nothing personal about it. Arvin Sloane was a man who did most of his work in his head, and left only the most minimal of paper trails.

Jack knew that from experience.

Sloane gestured. Jack settled into the leather-and-steel desk chair and gazed back at him. "I'm curious about the D.C. assignment," he said without further preamble. "There's more to that story."

Sloane favored him with the faintest of smiles. "I thought you might think so," he said. "It didn't go precisely as expected, did it?"

"Just what did you expect, Arvin?" Jack asked. He genuinely wanted to know.

"Not what Sydney and Dixon encountered," Sloane said. "I assure you of that. It was supposed to be a routine technical drill."

"Marshall does that kind of work well," Jack said. Irritation, barely held in check, made the words an accusation.

"Do you think the assignment was beneath Sydney in some way, Jack?" Sloane asked.

"Don't be ridiculous. The job is the job," Jack said. "I'm just wondering why, of all the assets available, you chose the one best able to deal with armed resistance."

Sloane smiled again. The expression enhanced the essentially neutral expression he nearly always wore, turning tranquility into complacency. "Don't be silly, Jack," he said. "You've been on the job too long for false modesty."

"We're talking about Sydney," Jack pressed.

"If the unexpected had to happen," the APO chief said, "we were fortunate to have someone on the scene who was so well qualified to deal with it."

"You know more than you're telling," Jack said, a wary tone in his voice. "We're supposed to be working together now."

"It was a routine maintenance assignment," Sloane said. "Background chatter indicates that a major arms shipment is in the offing. Information is the lifeblood of the work we do. You know that as well as I do."

"I know that information is something you don't share readily," Jack said. "And I don't like having Sydney sent into the field without the best possible briefing."

"She knew what she needed to know, Jack," Sloane said. "I value Sydney greatly, and would never expose her to unnecessary hazard."

"Experience has taught me to not trust your definition of 'unnecessary,'" Jack said.

"Danger comes with every assignment," Sloane said. "Surely you recognize that."

CHAPTER 4

The man in the picture had high cheekbones and dark eyes. Black hair, thick and neatly coiffed, framed clean-shaven features that were lean and sharply drawn. His skin was the color of weathered copper, and his narrow lips were set in a slight sneer. He looked like a caricature of a Spanish nobleman.

"This is Enrique Alcatena," Marshall said. He felt only slightly nervous standing before his teammates in the meeting room, wireless mouse clenched in one hand. "'Quique,' to his friends. But he's not our friend, so he's Enrique."

Seated at the table were Sloane, the two Bristows, and the rest of the APO team. Marshall, standing, was very aware that he was the center of attention, but just now he didn't mind. He was sufficiently comfortable with the subject of his briefing and was reasonably calm as he spoke. "What Enrique is, is me," he continued. "Or pretty much me. Or South America's version of me. Except—"

Sloane, at the head of the table, shot him a glance.

"Enrique Alcatena is a multi-technological expert. He's been something of a fixture in the South American intelligence community," Marshall continued.

"Which country?" Nadia asked. "That's a great deal of territory."

Marshall shook his head. "He's freelance, a consultant. He works for whomever pays the bills. The Secretaría de Inteligencia de Estado, the Agencia Nacional de Inteligencia, and like that." He pronounced each agency's name perfectly.

"Argentina and Chile," Nadia said.

Marshall nodded. "He's worked for most of the Spanish-speaking South American countries," he continued. "They seem to be his preferred customers, even though he's worked for other patrons too." He paused. "Never us, though—right?" he asked, directing his question to the head of the table.

"To the best of my knowledge," Sloane said. His tone of voice suggested that he didn't appreciate the question. "Please continue. Several of us have business after this meeting."

Marshall clicked the mouse again. The image of Enrique Alcatena was replaced with one of the button-size devices that Sydney had brought back from Washington. "I'm pretty sure Alcatena built this," he said. "Let me show you why."

He squeezed the mouse again, and another image appeared. It was the information tap, its cover removed to lie bare its interior. The picture was larger and offered enough detail to confuse the untrained eye. Hundreds of circuits were intertwined in elaborate patterns—gold-etched lines that met and formed nodes, then parted again to make new connections. Marshall knew that the elaborate electronic maze was encased in a host medium, but that medium was so optically transparent that the others were unlikely to even see it. The sum effect was of a three-dimensional golden tangle, many layers deep, with the efficient beauty shared by all good design work.

It was difficult to believe that someone had packed so much system into such a small device. The more he had studied Sydney's find, the more impressed Marshall had been. The size-complexity ratio was an order of magnitude greater than any he had encountered before.

"This is really, really nice work," he said as he realized that no one else seemed quite as awed. His teammates were exceptionally knowledgeable for laymen, but they lacked the technological insight to understand just how impressive the handiwork was. "This is the kind of thing that Señor Alcatena does best. He's probably the best in the world at making things small. I mean, I'm good, but this is better."

They were looking at him again instead of at the image. "Look," he said. Usually he was careful to use accessible language in a briefing like this one, but now, his enthusiasm gave free rein to technical terminology. "The conducting media are gold pseudo-polymers, only a hundred atoms or so wide. The sub-microchips were probably encoded with low-frequency—"

"Marshall," Sloane said, somewhere between a prompt and a warning.

He nodded again. "I spent a few hours comparing the inner works to archival materials. The monomolecular technology he used for execution is new, but the underlying design principles are the same. This is definitely an Alcatena product."

He sat back down, muttering, "Which raises some questions."

As if on cue, Eric Weiss stood. Marshall liked the affable man well enough, and felt mild envy at his easy self-assurance. He had worked closely with Weiss in identifying Alcatena, but the operations analyst had taken the ball and run with it. This wasn't research that Marshall would have felt comfortable doing himself.

"You probably noticed that Marshall referred to Alcatena mostly in the past tense," Weiss said. He scratched his nose. "It's not because he's dead. It's because he dropped completely out of sight about five years ago. I worked some resources in South America. Argentina and Chile weren't very forthcoming, but Brazil was; apparently, Alcatena never worked for them, and they still resent it. Word is that he retired." He paused and scratched his nose. "But we think someone made an offer sufficient to bring him back."

He clicked the mouse. The high-detail image that Marshall had left on display gave way to the slightly blurred image of a man of slight build, with narrow features and slicked-back hair. "Customs provided us with this. It's supposed to be one Eduardo Cortez, but facial-recognition software says it's Alcatena. Either way, the subject entered the United States six weeks ago, via Mexico. Homeland Security says the car he rented was turned back in at a Virginia agency and that 'Eduardo' left our country via Ronald Reagan National Airport."

Another click, and a briefing slide appeared, displaying columns of text and financial data. The dollar sums were enormous. "With the subject's entry date as a starting point, I took a look at international banking transactions. These three are clustered around that entry date—one a week before, one on the day, and one a week after. The name on the account is Eduardo's, but the Venezuela address makes it even more likely that we're talking about Alcatena."

"The security standards of Venezuelan banks?"

Vaughn asked, his words a bit of a surprise. He rarely interrupted at these meetings. "Very secure."

"Yeah, but what I was going to say is, they speak Spanish there," Weiss said. "And everything we have on him says that Alcatena shows strong preference for Hispanic culture. That may be why he's never worked for Brazil. I traced the payments back to Sweden, but the trail runs out at the issuing bank, Orten Haus. They're discreet." Weiss looked briefly unhappy, clearly disappointed to have met a dead end on the data trail. "*Very* discreet," he emphasized.

"Keep working that," Sloane said. "I'm familiar with Orten Haus. Their discretion is, shall we say, not absolute."

Weiss, already seated again, nodded.

"I think it's safe, then, to conclude that our Señor Alcatena has found a new patron," Sloane continued. He steepled his fingers and leaned back in his chair.

Marshall envied Sloane's air of utter calm and absolute, confident command. Sloane had long been a presence in Marshall's professional life, evolving from supervisor and even mentor, to hunted quarry, to tactical director. He had been the head of SD-6, and Marshall had obeyed his directives and had even curried favor with him. When the lie of SD-6 had been revealed, Marshall had transitioned to the CIA proper and joined in the hunt for his former supervisor. Now, sitting in a conference room and hearing Sloane's measured tones, he was only too aware of how much things had changed over the previous few years.

Sloane, remarkably, seemed in many ways not to have changed at all. Clearly, he felt none of the mingled déjà vu and wariness that Marshall felt, even now. It seemed to Marshall that Sloane was in some way the constant and the world was what had changed.

"I have some information," Sloane said. "Agency contacts in Washington report that the local police have taken into custody a man named Charles Kurilla. It seems they found him bleeding and unconscious in an alley off of K Street." He glanced in Sydney's direction. "He was dressed as a window-washer."

Sydney Bristow nodded, her features composed and neutral. "One of the response team," she said. "I knew that I'd wounded at least one. He must have gotten left behind."

"It seems likely," Sloane agreed. "Mr. Kurilla is proving a remarkably reticent customer, however. He's being held on suspicion, but he's not talking."

"I can have a word with him," Jack Bristow said. They were the first words he'd spoken since the meeting began. From past experience, Marshall knew that he likely wouldn't speak again.

"Excellent, Jack. But be discreet," Sloane said. He looked around the table, eyeing each operative briefly. Marshall found the gaze completely unfathomable. "I think we're at the leading edge of something, people. The tip of the iceberg and all that. I've secured authorization to investigate the situation more thoroughly. I'm sure you'll all be of great help, but I need you to be on your toes and ready to go."

Sydney Bristow did not so much squeeze the trigger as she stroked it. The big gun roared, bucking in her clenched hands and trying to knock her backward with its recoil, but she had braced herself well and stood steady. She fired again, and then a third and fourth time. In the enclosed space of the firing range, the shots were like thunder, beyond even the ability of the noise-blocking headset she wore to eliminate them completely. The back-flash of the pistol punched through the tinted lenses she wore and made black-fringed holes in her vision. She blinked to clear her eyes and waited for her hearing to return to normal.

Beside her in the firing-range lane, Vaughn slapped the recall button. Electric motors whirred, and the paper target made the long trip back to Sydney. It was the black silhouette of a man, stark against beige paper stock, with the kill-zones of head and heart indicated in red. Sydney's pistol fire had punched eight holes in it.

"Nice grouping," Vaughn said as he examined the sheet. At his side, Nadia nodded in agreement. Now that the echoes had faded, Sydney could hear him clearly. "Or groupings, I guess." Four holes marked the paper man's paper heart, and another three let light shine through his head. Vaughn indicated the eighth puncture, low on the imaginary man's neck. "This one's a little off," he said, pointing to the outlier.

"It's an unfamiliar weapon," Sydney said. She intended the words less as an excuse than as a simple statement of fact. She had qualified on every make, model, and caliber of firearm cleared for APO field use and more than a few that weren't, but this specific pistol was new to her. It was nothing special, a .44 magnum Desert Eagle, but every gun had its peculiarities.

Vaughn shook his head. A half-dozen ammunition clips lay on the small shelf at the head of the lane. He grabbed one at random and reloaded the gun. Assuming the proper stance, he raised the gun and fired four shots in rapid succession. He was bigger than Sydney but, even so, he clearly felt the recoil as much as she had.

Even before the target had returned again, Sydney could see that all four of Vaughn's shots had hit their marks. The target's paper heart hung in tatters.

"A poor workman and all that," Vaughn said, good-natured but still gently chiding. "It's not the gun. The gun's fine."

He had agreed to partner Sydney and Nadia for some practice on the APO range, but Sydney was beginning to wish that she had invited Dixon instead. Vaughn knew better than to be argumentative on a firing range, but his standards were high and he was matter-of-fact about voicing them.

That was to the good, she supposed. In a matter

like this, one should never let personal feelings stand in the way of telling someone what he or she needed to know.

"You pulled to the right on the last," Vaughn continued. "Right, and down."

"It's still a kill-shot," Sydney replied. The words came out more defensively than she had intended.

"Not as reliable, though," Vaughn said. He reloaded the gun and handed it to her. "You're trying too hard. Pick one target zone and stick with it. Don't try to be fancy. Just relax and let go."

Irritated, Sydney tried again. Even as she fired, she knew that allowing herself to feel even faintly annoyed was a mistake. It showed in the results. Six high-caliber bullets reduced the new target's center to confetti, but the surrounding, surviving paper showed that two rounds had missed their mark and fallen just outside the kill-zone. It was still world-class shooting, but not up to her usual standards.

Sydney said nothing as Vaughn inspected the final tally. He shook his head and half-smiled. "The idea," he said, "is to make the bullets go where you want them to go."

The words stung. "I know that," she said, even more sharply than before. "A missed shot is a wasted one."

"And a hazard," Vaughn said. "Maybe even to your own side."

Genuine anger colored her words now. "I know that. I know that stray rounds make trouble," she said, with sudden vehemence. "Don't *ever* tell me that I don't."

He looked at her wryly. "It's nothing personal, Syd," he said. "You asked me to play range-master for you two. It's part of the drill."

She nodded, and opened her mouth to say some more, but Nadia interrupted.

"It's still good shooting," Sydney's half sister interjected. "Higher than I'm rated."

Sydney glanced at her, grateful for the interruption. The conversation's currents had been heading toward troubled waters, and the casual comment did much to change that.

"You do fine," Vaughn said. He opened his PDA and scanned recent range scores. "There's room for improvement, but you do fine."

"There's always room," Nadia agreed easily. "Perhaps you could give me some pointers, then."

"I'll be happy to," Vaughn said. He scooped up another of the ammo clips and loaded the pistol yet again. As he handed it to Nadia, he said, "Just treat the gun like it's an extension of your body. This one is a real brute, but if you work *with* it, it'll work *for* you."

Sydney stood back and watched the two of them. She'd had enough shooting for one day, but she listened carefully to Vaughn's guidance. He was a great shot and a great teacher, methodical and supporting. She knew that he had been correct in his assessment of her earlier shooting.

Nadia was in stance now. She held the Desert Eagle at eye level, gripping it solidly with both hands. Vaughn stood behind her, his arms extended and his hands holding hers. "Excellent stance," he was saying. "Hold it securely, but not like you're try-ing to strangle it. Keep your wrists straight—"

The advice was all basic stuff, guidance that Sydney had heard hundreds of times before. Vaughn's "tips" were the same kinds of things that range-masters told their charges the world over. She had long since mastered and internalized them.

"Easy," Vaughn said. "Don't concentrate on

any single part of it. Just let the shot come naturally."

Nadia squeezed the trigger. The gun discharged four times in rapid succession, then paused as Nadia adjusted her stance. Another cascade of thunder came as she fired the second half of the clip. The entire sequence took less than five seconds.

Sydney's hearing returned to normal just in time to enable her to hear the whirring of the target return. She watched as Vaughn and Nadia inspected the perforated paper, and as her sometime-lover indicated the eight holes, one by one. They were grouped closely; not quite as close as Vaughn's or Sydney's groupings, but there were no outliers. All eight had fallen well within the red kill-zone. It was an excellent score, technically better than Sydney's, though the end result would have been the same in fieldwork.

"Syd," Vaughn said. He beckoned. "Come here. I think you've got some real competition."

"So I see," Sydney said, sincerely pleased and impressed. But even as she spoke, she could feel the faintest nibble of doubt.

What was she doing wrong?

CHAPTER 5

WASHINGTON, D.C.

The cops were both burly middle-aged men, African-American and overweight. One wore prescription lenses in black metal frames, and the other sported a neatly trimmed mustache. To Chuck Kurilla they looked like desk jockeys, and he was reasonably certain that he could have taken them both down. That is, he could have if his hands hadn't been shackled together and if there hadn't been a bandaged bullet hole in his left shoulder.

Neither officer had said anything to him since

they had pulled him out of the holding cell. They had put the cuffs on his wrists and led him down the long hallway to the interrogation room. Then, at last, their silence broke.

"Sit down," Glasses said, and pointed at the appropriate seat.

"I ain't talkin'," Chuck said as he dropped easily into the chair. Worn and wooden, it was still more comfortable than anything in his cell.

"So you've told us," Mustache replied.

"Stay there," Glasses said, just before the door slammed shut behind the two of them.

Chuck surveyed his surroundings, trying not to be too obvious about it. The interrogation room was pretty much the same as the seven others in his experience. Four walls, each about fifteen feet long, bounded a hard floor. Dead center in the room was a table big enough for six, but only two chairs flanked it. One was empty and the other, the one that held Chuck, faced a waist-level mirror about six feet wide. All of the furniture had been bolted to the floor.

Not for the first time, Chuck wished that the other members of his squad hadn't abandoned him when his wound had slowed him too much for the escape effort. He understood why they had and he would have done the same in their shoes, or worse, but he wished they hadn't. He wished very much that the cops hadn't found him.

"I ain't talkin'," he said again, this time for the benefit of whomever was behind the mirror. He rattled his cuffs a bit, testing their fit, and then shrugged. He knew how the police worked. They would come for him when they came. Until then, he might as well relax.

He had just slumped in the chair and begun to drum his fingers when the heavy door opened again and a man Chuck had never seen before entered. He might not recognize the man, but he recognized authority, and something made him respond to this man's air of power.

He wasn't especially tall or wide, but seemed big, somehow, solid and massive. He moved with easy grace; Chuck had seen mountain lions move like that. He had gray hair and steely eyes, and he gazed at Chuck with unnerving directness as he settled into the chair on the table's other side.

"There's no one behind the mirror," the man said. "We're alone." He said it as casually as if commenting on the weather or sports. For some reason, Chuck believed him.

"I ain't talkin'," Chuck said yet again. They were the only words that came to mind.

"Yes, you will," the man said, still with absolute assurance.

Again, Chuck believed him. Now, he could think of nothing to say.

The man set a leather portfolio on the table between them. He unzipped it and opened it like a book. One side held more zippered compartments, but the other was a clipboard carrying official-looking papers. The man appeared to study them.

"Kurilla," the man said. "That's Ukrainian, right?"

"I'm a good American," Chuck said sharply. "Born and bred." His foreign-sounding name had been a great source of embarrassment to him over the years.

"Uh-huh," said his visitor. He plucked a small card from his paperwork. "You gave this to the arresting officer. It sounds very official, but you need more than a slip of paper to exempt yourself from the jurisdiction of the United States government."

"From un-Constitutional laws and the authority of an improperly elected government," Chuck corrected him. He had memorized the words and their proper pronunciations. "Real Americans never knuckle under to tyrants."

"'Blue Mountain Boys,'" the man read from the card. "How long have you been in the citizens' militia, Kurilla?"

Chuck responded with his name and rank. He didn't believe in serial or Social Security numbers.

The big man shrugged. "I'll find out," he said.

"No," Chuck said, but this time, he could hear a quiver in his own voice. His visitor's absolute confidence was unnerving.

"The police doctor informs me that your wound is healing nicely and that you have no other health issues," the man said. "That's good." He unzipped another portfolio compartment.

The glass and chromed steel of a hypodermic needle glinted in the interrogation room's harsh light. Flanking the instrument were two ampoules of transparent fluid.

"You can't do this!" Kurilla said.

"There are many unpleasant things that people tell me I can't do," came the response. "Usually, I take no great pleasure in doing them, but this time, I don't mind.

"I really don't need to tell you this," the man continued as he filled the hypodermic. "But when I'm done here, you won't remember me or anything I've said, so I'll tell you. My name is Bristow. That was my daughter you tried to kill a few days ago."

He meant the Mexican-looking lady on the rooftop, Chuck realized. He recalled the woman's athletic moves and her skill with a pistol. His wounded shoulder throbbed at the memory, and the room suddenly felt colder.

What had he gotten himself into?

Bristow continued. "My knowing that makes this a lot easier."

Instinctively, Chuck tried to push back from the table, forgetting that the furniture was fixed and immobile. He tried to stand and get away, but the big man had already leaned across the table. One of Bristow's strong hands clamped down on his wrist. Chuck felt a biting sting as the needle slid home. "Not gonna talk," he said, words already slurring.

"Yes, you will," were the last words he heard before darkness claimed him.

CHAPTER 6

LOS ANGELES

It was a perfect day for a run. The sun was bright and the air was dry. The eternal Los Angeles summer was at its peak, with palm leaves and grass and foliage all intense shades of green under the cloudless blue sky.

Sydney wasn't the only one taking advantage of the weather. The course of her run took her through the park, past playing children and cuddling lovers, past a bustling volleyball game and a middle-aged woman playing catch with her dog. A cute guy wearing a striped muscle shirt and cut-off shorts jumped out of her way just in time to avoid collision, but he jumped with a smile and a wave.

Sydney smiled back at him. Most of her life was cloaked in secrecy, and anonymity was to be desired, but she didn't mind being noticed at times like this.

Her long legs pumped up and down in a loping run that devoured the distance. Breath came in steady, deep gulps and her muscles burned pleasantly. Her feet hit concrete sidewalk, then grass, then sidewalk again as she raced along.

The MP3 player hanging from her neck was loaded with an eclectic batch of techno, each selection with a good, driving beat. The tunes percolated in her earphones, masking out the noise and chatter of the everyday world. She could have been a player in a movie, with her own personal sound track.

The edge of the park approached. Without breaking pace, she turned and she passed through its gates, turning left onto the sidewalk. The walkway was crowded, but no one seemed to mind that Sydney continued her run unabated. People smiled and waved.

All was right in the world.

Five more minutes of easy galloping brought her back to her starting point. She slowed as she turned onto the walk, coming to an easy halt at the entrance of her home.

That was when she paused. The door was slightly ajar.

Sydney turned off the iPod. She pulled the earphones free, letting them hang from her neck like a doctor's stethoscope. She reached for the doorknob cautiously, but before her fingers reached it, the door swung back and open. A handsome young man stood framed in the opening.

"Hey," he said. "A good run?"

It was Danny, her fiancé. Since they had agreed to marry, he had been spending more and more time in her apartment. Sometimes, he acted as if he lived there.

Sydney liked that.

"Great," she said, leaning into the kiss he offered. Her arms embraced him, pulling him close, as if they would never let go. After a split second, her fiancé returned the embrace, hugging her tightly.

"A great run," Sydney said when they finally came up for air. "A wonderful day."

"All's right in the world, huh?" Danny asked with a grin. He stayed close to her as she entered, his arm looped easily around her waist. The half-embrace felt familiar and good.

"Yes," Sydney said. "The kind of day that you never want to end."

"Well, c'mon in and tell us all about it."

"Us?" Sydney asked.

"Yeah, us," Will Tippen said. She could see him now, sprawled on the big couch in front of the television. He was staring raptly at the glowing screen, at two squads of helmeted men who were waging a pitched and foolish battle over a football. With habitual disregard for his posture, Will had slid down on the couch far enough that he could balance a bowl of pretzels on his chest. He was nibbling one as he spoke.

"Hey you," Sydney said. She came up behind him and tousled his sandy hair. "Shouldn't you be working?"

"I'm at the library, doing hard-copy research," Will said easily. "Boy, this place sure is crowded. Heh."

A televised roar went up as someone made a touchdown.

With a delicate, ladylike snort of disbelief, Sydney returned her attention to Danny. "And you? Don't you have a lecture session this afternoon? Or has Will led you down the primrose path?"

"No," came the words. They were in another, feminine voice. "There was a power outage on campus. Everything's cancelled."

Sydney turned, just in time to see Francie emerge from the kitchen. "Be nice to Danny," her roommate said. "Or I'll take him away from you."

Sydney blinked in surprise.

Francie was carrying an open bottle of wine. She had several stemmed glasses trapped between the fingers of her left hand. With easy dexterity, she filled the first with ruby liquid and handed it to Danny. "Here, you," she said. "Let me do the corrupting."

Sydney stared at her as Francie filled a second glass and offered it to her. The other woman's face opened in a wide grin and her dark eyes sparkled. "Drink?" she asked. "Or do you want to cool down first?"

Fingers numb, Sydney accepted the glass but did not sip. The happiness of a moment before, pure and simple and unalloyed, had vanished and she had no idea why. All that she knew was that something was terribly wrong, and that, she knew with a dreadful certainty.

"What's wrong, Syd?" Francie asked. The tall, African-American woman smiled. "You look like you've seen a ghost."

"Hey! If you're not going to drink that, I will," Will said. He scrambled to his feet and reached for the wineglass in Sydney's hand.

"You—you're not supposed to be here," Sydney said slowly, still staring at her roommate. She felt very cold.

"What do you mean?" Francie asked, puzzled. "This is my home too."

Will's fingers touched Sydney's glass. Sydney's fingers opened. The glass fell, shattering on the floor. Red wine splashed in all directions.

"Sydney!? What is it? What's wrong?" Danny asked.

Francie made a sound of alarm. "Look!" she said. "You've gotten wine everywhere!" She knelt to pick up the broken glass and looked up at Sydney.

There was wine on her face.

No. The liquid wasn't wine.

It was blood.

An oozing bullet hole had opened on Francie's forehead. Red rivers ran from it, down her face. Sydney gasped.

"What's wrong?" Francie asked. "Why are you looking at me like that?"

More wounds erupted across her chest. A line of bullet holes blossomed, red flowers that leaked and bubbled.

Francie asked the question again. The words came very slowly, and echoed as if heard from a great distance. "What's wrong?"

Sydney felt the scream building inside her.

"What's wrong?" This time, the voice was nearby and the words were clear and precise, even if a little sleepy-sounding.

Sydney's mouth had filled with a metallic taste and her heart pounded. The bedsheets, a messy tangle now, were cold and clammy with her own sweat. A wave of nausea swept through her and she shivered.

She recognized the symptoms even as they began to fade. This was classic flight-or-fight stuff, the aftermath of an adrenaline rush that came with instinctive fear. It had been years since Sydney had felt the effect so profoundly. Training and experience had long blunted panic's edge.

That edge had just proven that it could still cut, however, and cut deeply.

The light that spilled in from the hallway defined Nadia's familiar silhouette, then splashed across Sydney's bed. Lit from behind, her face in shadows, Nadia's expression was impossible to read, but her voice showed great concern.

Sydney rubbed her eyes. She forced herself to speak calmly. "Just a bad dream," she said.

Nadia nodded. "You cried out," she said. She sounded fully awake now.

"God," Sydney said, still panting. "I woke you?"

"Yes," Nadia said.

"I'm sorry."

"What was the dream about?" her roommate asked.

"I—I don't remember," Sydney said slowly. "I almost never remember my dreams."

For a long minute, she was very aware of Nadia's steady, appraising gaze. Then, the other woman nodded again. "All right. I'm going back to bed, Sydney," she said. "I hope you sleep well."

"I hope so too," Sydney said with ready honesty.

After Nadia had closed the door again, Sydney lay back on her bed and stared at the ceiling. Her room was dark, but she didn't mind that. The darkness helped her think.

She had lied to Nadia, at least at little. The dream had, indeed, faded, but not completely. Her mind's eye was filled with a single, unsettling image. She saw Francie, bearing the stigmata of the wound that had killed her, as well as of the wounds that had killed Allison Doren, the woman who had been her killer, replacement, and impostor.

Sydney knew how dreams worked. The subject had come up more than once in counseling sessions and in college readings. Dreams could be messages from the subconscious to the conscious mind, deeply encoded or maddeningly blatant.

Why was she dreaming about her dead roommate? The question seemed to have no answer. Sydney pulled the sheets closer around her body for warmth and tried to sleep.

Dawn was long in coming.

CHAPTER 7

VIRGINIA

The mountain road they traveled was little more than packed dirt, rutted and raw, a twisted path that ran though densely wooded landscape. It would be a challenge to any vehicle's suspension system, and the big Humvee rocked and shook as it rolled along.

"This is old-growth forest," the driver said, both hands firmly gripping the steering wheel. He was a wiry man, with dark hair that peeked out from under a billed baseball-type cap. The cap, like the windbreaker he wore, bore the letters ATF on one breast.

On the other was the seal of the Bureau of Alcohol, Tobacco and Firearms. "Some of these trees date back to the Civil War."

In the passenger seat was Jack Bristow, gazing out the windshield at the early morning sky as he sipped coffee from the thermos cup he held. Jack said nothing. He had never been much for small talk.

The driver pretended that he was. "Ever been back here before?" he asked, making it a direct question.

Jack shook his head. Taciturn was one thing and rude was another, especially when dealing with an ally. "No. Can't say that I have."

"Old growth," the driver said again. "The culture back here is old too. You don't think of Virginia as being a wild state, but these parts are. A lot of the locals don't recognize the federal government at all. A lot of 'em are off the books—born at home, no Social Security number, no tax ID. Homeschooled, if they're schooled at all.

"Think that's one reason the Blue Mountain Boys get away with so much. Folks around here have a very local mindset, and the Boys are as local as they come. They run this part of the county like they own it."

Jack sipped more coffee. It wasn't very good, but it was hot and the caffeine was welcome. He had been awake for much of the night. After his D.C. interrogation of Kurilla, he had engaged in some fairly complex behind-the-scenes interagency negotiations, including some string-pulling facilitated by CIA HQ in Langley. Then he had driven some three hours down Routes 66 and 81 to the Shenandoah Valley and the rendezvous that he had so carefully arranged. Another hour of travel had followed, along progressively less well paved roads that led into the more remote reaches of the Blue Ridge Mountains. Jack was still energized and aware, but he was tired of the road and tired of the ATF agent's chatter.

The coffee didn't help much.

"They're basically good people, most of the locals," the man said. He shifted gears and turned onto what looked like a dirt trail through the woods. "Family folks." He glanced at Jack. "You got family, sir?"

"Just the one," Jack said, surprising himself a bit with the disclosure; he almost never spoke of his private life. He'd been thinking about Sydney a great deal for much of the day, since he had reviewed her marksmanship scores at the APO range. He supposed that having her on his mind had made him respond.

He made a mental note not to share any more personal information with his driver.

The ATF agent nodded. "Family, it's all that really matters," he said. Then, after a moment's silence, he continued. "Almost there," he said, and unhooked a walkie-talkie from above the windshield. He glanced at Jack again. "Cell phones don't work here. We're miles off any commercial network. But I guess you already found that out for yourself."

Jack nodded. He was accustomed to ready connectivity, at least on the domestic front, and the lack of it now felt strange. He had been in such situations before, of course, but only rarely on the domestic front. He felt as if he were somewhere other than the United States, or as if he had traveled back in time.

The Humvee slowed as the driver spoke into the portable radio. "Clarion to base," he said. "I have my passenger. Status?"

After a few additional exchanges, staccato and jargon-riddled, he broke the connection and returned the radio to its rack. "Looks like we missed most of the excitement," he said. "The raid went off on schedule, just before dawn."

"I'll live," Jack answered sourly. The information didn't please him, but it wasn't any surprise, either. There had been no assurances that the ATF forces on scene would delay the raid for his arrival. That was reasonable. A field commander had to set his own priorities. Jack would have liked to be there for the actual encounter, but what was done was done.

The forest gave way to a clearing. At the far end was a long, low shed that backed up to the raw rock of a cliff side. Between their vehicle and the shed, in the clearing proper, were more Humvees. Another four men, clad in Army-style fatigues and with their hands cuffed behind them, sat in the bare dirt of the clearing. Surrounding them were more men in ATF jackets and caps. They stood with guns drawn and rifles at ready, clearly standing guard. Jack counted ten agents. The fresh welcoming air of the woods took on the tang of tear gas.

They had, indeed, missed the excitement.

The Humvee came to a stop. An agent holstered his weapon and came forward to receive them. Jack was pleased to note that several of the others watched attentively. These men were professionals.

"John Santangelo," the man said as they shook hands. Clearly of Italian descent, he managed to look genial and slightly sinister at the same time. "Agent in charge. You must be our observer."

"That's right," Jack said, and handed Santangelo the credentials of the day. "Joe Gill, DEA. How's business?"

Santangelo looked disgusted. "It could have gone a lot better. We were looking for the big guns, but they were missing in action," he said. He indicated the four prisoners. "These are small fry, the roaches who didn't move fast enough when the kitchen lights came on."

"Ain't gonna talk," one of the handcuffed men said. His voice had the same country twang as Kurilla's.

"Shut up," replied one of the guards.

"I need a look around," Jack said, ignoring the exchange. "This site came up in a case I'm working. My boss wanted me to follow up."

"Well, come on, then," Santangelo said. "I'll show you the homestead." He glanced at the driver.

"You and the others wait out here. Keep an eye on our friends with the wrist jewelry and see to it that Mr. Gill and I aren't disturbed."

The shed that the ATF had raided was built long and low, and basic in construction and entirely functional in design. It had been built to enclose as much space as possible, as quickly practically as possible. Floorboards creaked as the two men stepped inside.

Within was a complex network of distilling equipment. Fermentation units, boilers, and condensing coils were all linked by long loops of metal tubing. Outside, the morning air had been cool, but in here it was oppressively hot, as much from the heat of fermentation as from the boilers' operation. The stink of tear gas was still heavy in the air, but underlying it now was the sweeter aroma of corn whiskey. Jack and Santangelo were alone in the place.

"Designer hooch," Santangelo said in disgust. "Trendy stuff. End-users pay $100 a quart to say they've got the real deal. The money goes to fund the Blue Mountain Boys."

"Is that all?" Jack asked, after a cursory inspection. He saw nothing out of the ordinary for such operations.

"Just moonshine," Santangelo said. "No methamphetamine." He paused. "If that's really what you're looking for."

Jack looked at him. "We got a tip," he said.

"I've been running operations in this neck of the woods for ten years now," Santangelo said. He shook his head. "I keep my ear to the ground. I've never heard of the Blue Mountain Boys dealing in crank. Protection rackets, a bit of gun-running, yeah. But no meth."

Jack said nothing.

"You're a Fed, but if my wife let me bet, I'd bet six months' pay that you aren't DEA," he continued. "And that your name's not Joe Gill, no matter what it says on your card."

"Oh?" Jack said. He felt no particular concern, but a grudging respect. From the look and sound of things, Santangelo was a man who knew what he was doing, and Jack valued competence. Besides, it didn't really matter that the other man knew who his employer wasn't, as long as he didn't know who that employer *was*. "Well, we can worry about that another time. What happens here when we're done?"

"Impound the equipment, destroy the stock, and level the facility. The usual drill," Santangelo said.

"Let's look in the basement first," Jack said.

"The basement?" Santangelo asked blankly.

Jack moved to the rear of the moonshine factory. The back was like the rest of the structure, sturdy beams that anchored rough planks. He rapped on the unfinished wood, one plank at a time, until he found the section that sounded hollow.

Santangelo was watching him carefully. An expression of mingled realization and disgust was forming on his broad features. Clearly, he had guessed what Jack already knew.

"Don't beat yourself up about this. You would have found it sooner or later," Jack said. He slapped the wall. "I need to break through this."

Kurilla had told him of dummy nails and wall planks that could be removed with a few minutes' effort, but Jack didn't feel like bothering. When Santangelo handed him a fireman's ax, he swung it almost immediately. There was something satisfying about the work. Chunks of wood flew in all directions, and as he kicked the last splintered boards aside, the rock wall that the shed had been built flush against lay revealed.

So was the hole that gaped in it. It was the mouth of a cavern. It was deep and dark, and led far into the mountain's interior. Water dripped in the distance, and cool air spilled from the newly revealed opening.

The two men stepped into the dank coolness and surveyed it slowly. Someone had taken the time and trouble to lay a wooden floor in the cave's front area. A flashlight from Santangelo's belt showed other signs of Man in the hidden place. A dozen wooden crates of varying sizes, a small worktable and a chair, and other mundane furnishings had been scattered untidily about. But for the condensation-slimed rock walls and roof, and for the steady drip-drip-drip of water in the distance, they could have been in a warehouse.

"I should have known," Santangelo said softly. "These hills are lousy with caves. They make great caches."

Jack didn't bother to answer. His essential dislike of small talk had reasserted itself. He popped the tops of two crates, chosen at random from a dozen identical ones.

Each held twenty Russian-make assault rifles.

"Seems the Blue Mountain Boys don't believe in buying American," Santangelo said. He knelt to examine the find. "Some patriots. This many guns, you're in business to sell them. So the moonshine operation was a cover?"

"Maybe," Jack said. "A profitable one."

"I'd better get my guys in here."

"They can wait," Jack said. "And I don't think this is merchandise. It may be payment."

"You talk like a man who knows," Santangelo said.

Offering an explanation seemed both unnecessary and unwise. The interview with Kurilla had provided specific information that fit neatly with what was already known about the operations of groups like the Blue Mountain Boys, and it seemed reasonably likely that Santangelo would fill in the blanks himself. Rather than say anything, Jack busied himself investigating the remainder of items stored in the finished portion of the cave.

Most of it was of little interest. The other crates held more guns, rounds of ammunition, combat rations, and other oddments that a so-called citizens' militia would find useful. Everything was thoroughly conventional. A drawer in the worktable held some moderately interesting maps and paperwork.

And something else.

Jack fixed Santangelo with a steady gaze.

"Earlier, you were right," he said. "My name isn't Gill, and I'm not DEA."

The other man's answer was a simple nod, less of agreement than of acceptance.

"And I can count on your discretion, right?" Jack asked.

"Certainly, Mr. Gill," Santangelo said. Now, he was smiling very slightly. "I believe in inter-agency cooperation."

"Good," Jack said, and lifted a pistol from the drawer.

He had never seen anything like it before. It was small and light, little more than an *L*-shaped piece of gray plastic that could fit almost entirely inside his hand. In design, it looked like a child's toy, with smooth, futuristic lines. It had no muzzle opening, and where the trigger should have been, there was a small, recessed button.

Santangelo reached for it, obviously curious. Rather than pass it to him, Jack raised the gun and test-fired it at a cavern wall.

There was no sound, no visible discharge from the device, but the moist rock erupted in sparks and steam. As the light show faded, Jack pressed the button again.

"Nothing," Santangelo said.

"Nothing," Jack agreed. The single shot had been the gun's last, or only.

He examined his target. The stone was warm to the touch, and dry where its cloak of condensation had boiled away, but otherwise undamaged.

"Looked like what happens when you put foil in a microwave oven," Santangelo said.

"Yeah," Jack said. Santangelo's words had echoed his own thoughts. The cave walls were rich in metallic salt deposits that he knew fluoresced under microwave exposure, which explained the sparking. That the stone was undamaged didn't surprise him, but he wondered what such a handgun would do to a human being. He dropped the weapon into his coat pocket and gave Santangelo back his flashlight.

"You're right," he said. "No crystal meth here. Thanks for the hospitality, Agent Santangelo. You'd better get your guys in here to secure this contraband you found. Good job."

"Hah," the ATF agent said easily. "Glad to be of service, Mr. Gill." He paused. "Why do you suppose they had only one—of those?"

"Don't know," Jack said. "But I'll find out."

LOS ANGELES

"—can take as much as twenty-four hours for major transaction records to propagate through the financial networks, and much longer for small ones," Weiss said. He referred to his notes. "Between that and Venezuela's attention to privacy concerns for banking customers—"

"For *affluent* banking customers," Sloane corrected him, interrupting from his habitual seat at the head of the table. He toyed with a pencil as he spoke, whether from boredom or agitation, Sydney couldn't tell.

Either way, it was mildly surprising. Sloane almost never fidgeted.

"Affluent clients, yes," Weiss agreed. "And as such things go, Alcatena has had a busy six months. We've identified some very interesting purchases made on the accounts identified earlier. Gold microfilaments, prototype sub-microchips, power cells."

Beside Sydney, Marshall sat up to attention, noticeably more interested. He was always interested in technological data. He opened his mouth to speak, but Sydney shook her head almost imperceptibly in warning. It was one thing for Sloane to interrupt a report, and quite another for Marshall.

Unimpeded, Weiss soldiered on. "We were able to trace the deliveries to an address in southern Peru. Essentially, we've tentatively identified Alcatena's current base of operations."

"And we'd like very much to know what he's up to these days," Sloane said as Weiss sat again. "I think it's safe to say that he's aligned with the arms deal that interests our friends at K so much. Someone has paid him enough to come out of retirement, and enough to fund dramatic advances in his technologies. I'd like very much to know who that someone is." He looked around the table. "Your operational directives—"

The door opened. Jack Bristow entered and, with a nod of greeting, seated himself in the remaining empty chair. That was a surprise too. Her father was habitually prompt, and if he missed a meeting now and then, he had never before arrived at one late.

"Ah, Jack," Sloane said. He didn't seem surprised by the tardiness. "How was your flight?"

"Late," came the response. "But the trip as a whole was successful." With a nod to Sloane, he passed a large interdepartmental mail envelope across the table. "This is for you," he said.

Marshall immediately unwound the red string of its fastener and upended the envelope. What looked like a toy pistol fell out, and Marshall looked at it closely. "It looks like a phaser," he said, curling his fingers around its grip.

"Jack?" Sloane said. The patience in his voice was too obvious to be sincere.

In clipped, succinct sentences, Jack Bristow summarized his visit to Washington and beyond. He summarized his interview with the incarcerated Charles Kurilla, his coordination with DEA and ATF resources, and his trip to rural Virginia. His download was as orderly and precise as any written report that Sydney had ever read, and he spoke without any reference to notes or backup materials.

"Blue Mountain Boys?" Vaughn asked when the senior agent had finished. The name fell outside his expertise.

"A minor regional citizens' militia," Jack said. "This one is evidently motivated less by ideology than by a general fondness for dressing up like soldiers and firing guns." He indicated the futuristic weapon as Marshall busily examined it with evident delight. "My guess is, K-Directorate is using them for grunt work, either because they're expendable or for deniability. I read and memorized some paperwork about that, too, but I can provide details later."

Sloane was looking at the gun. A look of subtle familiarity was on his face. Sydney was certain that he had seen the weapon before and that he was surprised to see it now. That was significant. It wasn't easy to take Arvin Sloane by surprise.

"The info fits in with what we know already," Weiss said. He looked puzzled. "Is that some kind of toy?" he asked, pointing at the futuristic pistol.

"I think that's more of Alcatena's work," Jack said as Marshall nodded in agreement. "I found it in Virginia. It seems to fire microwaves of some sort." He described the effects of firing it in the militia's outpost.

Now, Marshall looked puzzled. "Microwaves?" he said, and shook his head, staring into the little gun's muzzle. "Well, if you say so, but—well, the configuration is all wrong for any substantive output."

"We can talk about that later," Sloane interjected. He shifted his gaze from the pistol to the older Bristow. "As Weiss explained, before your arrival, he seems to have located Señor Alcatena."

"Where is he?" Jack asked.

"Southern Peru," Weiss said. "Cuzco."

It seemed appropriate. Cuzco was one of the oldest cities in the Western Hemisphere, home first to Indians and then to the early Spanish settlers. People there lived and worked in buildings five hundred or more years old, and tourists used it as a staging area for visits to Machu Picchu, the "lost city of the Incas." Rich in history, Cuzco made perfect sense as a base of operations for someone of Alcatena's cultural preferences.

Sloane nodded. "I want all hands ready to move at a moment's notice," he said. "Sydney—you, Nadia, and Dixon should plan on being out of the country for a day or two." He indicated Flinkman. "I'm certain Marshall will provide you with any findings he makes before you embark. I'll meet with you each personally once operational orders have been cut."

As the other members of assembled team stood to leave, Sydney approached him. "You're good at hiding things," she said. When he looked at her quizzically, she continued. "That's not an accusation, just an honest assessment."

Sloane smiled. It was the accepting smile of a man who had received a compliment. The others had filed out of the meeting room, and they were alone now. If he had seemed busy and had even multitasked a moment before, he appeared entirely focused on her now.

Sydney continued. "Good, but not perfect. I saw you react when you saw that toy gun. You've seen it before."

"No," Sloane said, pleasantly enough.

"Something that looked like it, then," Sydney said. When he didn't reply, she pressed the issue. "You recognized *something*."

"We haven't always worked together, Sydney. It doesn't please me that we've not always been on the same side, but it's the truth," Sloane said with a nod. "I've seen things you haven't and have done things you don't know about."

She looked at him without comment. To say that they hadn't always been on the same team struck her as a grotesque oversimplification of Sloane's complex network of deceit and betrayal.

"Your father's find is not one of those things, I assure you," Sloane said. "But as Marshall recognized some of the design work on the signal tap, I recognize some of the pistols' design work."

"Why not tell him, then?" she asked sharply. "What are you hiding?"

He had to be hiding something.

Sloane shook his head almost imperceptibly. "I don't want to direct Marshall down any misleading paths," he said. "I'll add my input to his findings when the time is right."

"Fair warning," Sydney said. "I'll hold you to that."

"Please do," Sloane said. He paused. "Sydney, should I assign other assets to this operation?"

"What?" she asked, startled. "No! Why?"

He looked at her with great concern in his tired eyes. "During the meeting, I noticed your attention wandering. You seem fatigued," he said. "Are you sleeping well?"

"I'm fine, and I'm ready," she said, with some heat. "Spare me the crocodile tears. *I'm* not the one with a guilty conscience."

CHAPTER 8

PERU

Birkenstock sandals sounded like horse hooves as they struck the hard cobblestones. Their staccato clatter echoed against storefronts and windows before being lost in the cool Peru night. A blond woman, lithe and athletic, and her companion made their way across the broad square that was the heart of ancient Cuzco. By day, this concourse would have been hot and busy. Eager vendors would have contended for the attention of tourists. If the market square was the city's heart, the tourists were its lifeblood. Casually and without a second thought, they could spend more in an hour than most locals could earn in a week, and in return, they enjoyed near-total safety. No one accosted or robbed Cuzco's guests; they were too valuable ever to threaten.

Now, however, the traffic was lighter by orders of magnitude. Music drifted from the nearby taverns and restaurants and open-air cafés, and the occasional shop still played host to patrons along the square's perimeter, but the broad central area was nearly empty. Most tourists had retired to the hotels and hostelries, to rest and prepare for daytime visits to the many local ruins. Most natives had returned home, to rest and prepare for another day of bargaining and sales. Nearly everyone who hadn't retired for the day was busily drinking beer or eating local dishes.

The blond woman was tall and moved with easy grace. Her attire was an expensive mix of traditional and designer fashion. A patterned kerchief held her hair up and away from her face so that it ran in a honey-color waterfall down her shoulders and back. A traditional shawl warmed her shoulders, but rather than humble wool, this garment had been woven of expensive cashmere, like the peasant blouse beneath it. Her skirt was of silk, and she wore copious silver and turquoise jewelry that incorporated ankhs, stars, crescent moons, and other quasi-mystic symbols.

In short, she looked less worldly than other-worldly.

"Feel the atmosphere!" she told her companion in a high, girlish voice. "Feel it! This is just like my spirit-guide said it would be!"

The bulky black man walking beside her made no reply. He was dressed more formally, in a dark suit and light shirt, with his collar secured by a clasp rather than a tie. There was a bulge under the left arm of his jacket.

"I've lived here before! I *know* I have!" the blond woman said. "Maybe it was after France. It would have had to be after France, wouldn't it?"

"I don't know, ma'am," the man said with obvious patience.

"When was Marie Antoinette, you know, un-headed?" she asked.

"The queen of France met her fate in 1793, ma'am," he said. Two Scandinavian women, taller and blonder, approached the pair. To judge by their looks, they were tourist stragglers, and harmless.

Nonetheless, the black man moved to put himself between them and his charge. As they passed, one woman whispered something to the other and they both laughed. Clearly, they had overheard the discussion of past lives.

"You're making an impression, Syd," Dixon said, sotto voce.

She acted as if she hadn't heard. "Okay, okay, if I died in 1793 and my chi passed to another vehicle, that could have been here, couldn't it?"

"You were Clara Barton after you were Marie Antoinette," Dixon said, back in character. He was striking a delicate balance in his responses, offsetting a personal assistant's responsiveness with an intelligent man's skepticism. "Clara Barton was born in 1821."

"That leaves, um, twenty-eight years in between," Sydney said, still speaking in character. She was a California show business heiress, an eager believer in New Age mysticism. "Maybe I didn't last very long. Maybe I had an adventure and that's why I respond so strongly to this place."

"Perhaps." Dixon moved to Sydney's other side, again putting himself between her and a passerby. His cover was as her personal security consultant and translator, which gave him a very good reason to be armed.

"Well, it makes perfect sense to me," she said, sounding breathless and naive. "Did Cuzco have a lady president back then? I must have been someone important. All my past lives are important."

"Of course, ma'am," Dixon said. His infinite patience had begun to sound slightly less infinite. He gestured at a secluded lane that parted from the market square. "I believe we should go left here."

Sydney continued her chatter as they walked past a tavern, a souvenir stall, and a florist's shop. At night, with the windows shuttered, many of the buildings here could have been plucked from another century. They were low and stolid, few of them more than one-story tall, and built of stone blocks that had become weathered and rounded with age. The sidewalks were broad flagstones that offered better purchase to Sydney's impractical shoes.

Only a few windows remained lit at this hour. They drew up short before one, a segmented-glass expanse fronting a small commercial gallery. On display in the window were pottery, small tapestries, and vividly stylized paintings. Sydney drummed with perfectly manicured nails on the gallery window.

"Here it is," she chirped. She read the big letters of the sign above the window. "'Muñoz.' Tell me what the rest of it says."

Dixon obliged readily. Anyone witnessing would immediately realize that he was her needed translator. "'Licensed export of fine antiques,'" he said, translating from the Spanish. "'Agent for local artists. Rare artifacts. Carlos Muñoz, proprietor.'"

"Yes!" Sydney said. "This is it!" She seemed almost giddy as Dixon opened the door for her. "This must be the place!"

The interior of the gallery was large and low. It was also crowded, striking a tentative balance between the owner's need to have wares on hand and the need to display those wares efficiently. Tables, shelving units, and wall niches presented scores of intriguing items. Books, bric-a-brac, and statuary shared displays. Tapestries hung like curtains from the ceiling, serving as partitions to segregate works by age or theme. Another tapestry screened off the rear of the establishment, presumably hiding storage or workspace. A man with strong Indian features looked up from a matched set of granite bowls and greeted them effusively. "Good evening!" he said in perfect English. "May I help you?"

Sydney looked at Dixon, making a great show of surprise. He looked back at her, less effusive. She turned back to Muñoz. "You speak American?" she asked.

"How may I help you?" he asked again, with oily politeness.

"I'm looking to buy one of those crystal skulls," Sydney said eagerly.

"Crystal skulls?" the man said blankly.

"Yes! The sacred talismans of ancient Incan magic," Sydney said, oblivious to his confusion.

"I have no skulls here," the man said.

Sydney leaned close. She whispered conspiratorially. "You know," she said. "The *crystal* skulls. You can tell me. I'm a friend of Shirley's."

"Who is this Shirley?" the man asked.

"Look, can we just speak to Mr. Muñoz?" Sydney asked.

"I am Muñoz," he replied.

"Then you know about the sk-u-u-lls!" she said, stretching the word until it was several syllables long. This kind of role was almost impossible to overplay. The object of the exercise was to demand attention and annoy so that their host would be relieved when he no longer had to deal with her.

"The lady is interested in purchasing antediluvian occult artifacts," Dixon interjected. His explanation didn't seem to help.

Muñoz attempted again to explain that he had no crystal skulls of any vintage on hand. Halfway through his explanation, the door to the gallery opened again and another woman entered. Well-dressed and wearing tastefully chosen jewelry, she was younger than Sydney, and shorter with darker hair. She had luminous eyes that flashed as she approached Muñoz and spat a series of syllables at him.

"*¿Que?*" the gallery host asked, puzzled. The words had been neither English nor Spanish.

Nadia railed at him again. Her tirade was fast-paced and guttural, and she accentuated many of her incomprehensible comments with angry gestures. She leaned close and prodded Muñoz's chest with one index finger. Her breath was heavy with alcohol.

"She wants to know why you cheated her husband on the serigraphs," Dixon interjected, still in character.

Muñoz looked at him blankly. "You understand her?" he asked.

He nodded. "She's speaking Czech," he said. "I'm a professional translator. It's one of my languages." The language had been chosen carefully as one that Nadia could manage and that no one on-site at the gallery was likely to understand.

Nadia ranted some more. She gestured angrily, her fingertips grazing an antique lyre perched precariously on a display unit. The wooden instrument toppled at the contact, and Muñoz yelped in dismay.

"She's drunk!" he said, grabbing the lyre before it could hit the floor. "These things—they are very valuable! I can't have her here like this!"

Dixon said something. Nadia looked at him. She spoke more words in Czech, directed at him this time. She smiled ingratiatingly and toyed with the collar of his jacket.

"She—she seems to like you," Muñoz said. The shrew of a moment before had become mildly ingratiating instead, and he was clearly relieved.

Nadia leaned back a bit, half-draping herself on a shelving unit. It shook, and books spilled to the floor. She extended one foot and toyed with the cuff of Dixon's left pants leg.

"She seems to," Dixon agreed.

"Can—can you help me?" Muñoz asked. He was thoroughly focused on the more annoying of his patrons now.

A brief exchange between Dixon and Nadia ensued. She giggled flirtatiously as Dixon shook his head, and then translated her words for the benefit of their host.

"She says her husband purchased for her a series of limited-edition prints from you two days ago," Dixon told him. More Czech spilled from Nadia's lips. "She says that she had the prints professionally appraised in Lima and that they're trash. She wants her money back."

Muñoz looked confused. He denied the accusation, and denied ever having served a Czech customer at all. Nadia, through her interlocutor, pressed the issue. As Dixon relayed her words, her voice started to creep up in volume again, despite soothing comments by the two men.

Sydney left the three of them like that. Dixon and

Nadia were good at what they did, and she could tell that they were having fun with the assignment. They could keep Muñoz occupied as long as necessary.

She edged away from them slowly, drifting toward a corner display of religious icons that combined Indian imagery with elements of the Catholic faith. They were precisely the kind of thing that would attract her cover identity. Before she reached them, she ducked behind one partitioning curtain and then another. Even she was surprised at how easily she had broken the line of sight without Muñoz even noticing. He was still too busy with her half sister to bother with the ditzy American.

The gallery's back room was cluttered and dirty, and musty like a warehouse. A quick survey showed Sydney nothing of promise. The walls that bounded it were another matter. They were made of centuries-old blocks of dark stone, like the rest of the gallery's walls. But for the bare lightbulbs that hung from the ceiling, the place looked nearly unchanged from the days when Spanish colonists had made it their home.

The only other indication of modern occupancy was a heavy security door and frame set solidly in ancient wall, with a key-card reader in its frame.

Sydney carried a small assortment of high-tech burglar tools. She selected an electronic pass-card, Marshall Flinkman's version of a skeleton key, and used it. The steel door whisked open, revealing a narrow flight of stone stairs. Without a second thought, Sydney headed down them, into the gloom below. Nadia had entered the gallery two minutes earlier. Between them, she and Dixon could keep Muñoz safely diverted for twice that long. She was relatively safe for the moment. She had enough time to inspect the lay of the land.

If the gallery's interior was a holdover from times past, the world beneath it could have been a prophecy of the future. The ceiling was low, but finished in acoustical tile and modern lighting fixtures. Under their soft fluorescent glow, banks of electronic equipment gleamed. Two spotlessly clean workbenches held precisely arrayed tools and pieces of equipment in various stages of assembly. The length of one wall housed black-finished cabinets that Sydney recognized as file servers, linked to the outside world by heavy cables that disappeared into spaces between that wall's component blocks.

Paydirt!

Sydney wore a brooch in the form of an ankh, the ancient Egyptian symbol of life and fertility. She unfastened it from her blouse and pressed it to one of the server cabinets, where it clung. She pressed the turquoise oval at its center. The recording device hidden there clicked once, so softly that she felt rather than heard it, and went to work. This was a refinement and elaboration of a familiar Flinkman device. It could access and copy electronic memories via wireless links, and its size gave it enormous data capacity.

Leaving the ankh to do its work, Sydney moved around the hidden workroom quickly. The heavy silver and turquoise necklace she wore held a hidden camera, and she used it to capture images of the hardware on display.

Weiss's research had borne good fruit. The toolsets included magnifying loupes and micro-fine tweezers, and spools of what looked like golden spiderweb strands. The partially assembled systems had to be Alcatena's work.

But where was the inventor himself?

Sprawled on the floor behind one workbench was the answer. It was the corpse of a man with high cheekbones. Black hair framed features that were lean and sharply drawn. Even paled by death, his skin was the color of weathered copper.

His eyes were gone.

Sydney smothered a gasp as she saw the extent of the damage. The dark eyes that had glared so recently at her from a briefing slide at APO headquarters were ruined craters now, burst from within. The skin that surrounded them was reddish and rippled, presumably damaged by whatever had destroyed his eyes. Sydney pressed her fingers to the dead man's forehead, assessing his temperature. He had been dead for at least a day.

"He has been dead for thirty-six hours," someone said from behind her. "I have waited for you that long."

Sydney froze.

"Turn around slowly," the familiar voice continued. "If you feel no concern for your own safety, consider that of your friends'."

She turned. Midway down the staircase stood the man who had introduced himself as Carlos Muñoz. Some five feet behind him were Dixon and Nadia, their hands clasped atop their heads. Behind the two APO agents were two hard-faced men Sydney had never seen before, but she recognized the type easily enough. Someone had trained Muñoz and his men well enough that they kept a safe distance from their charges but were close enough to use their weapons.

Those weapons were gray pistols, futuristic in design and small enough to be hidden almost completely in a man's hand. They were precise matches for the weapon that Jack Bristow had recovered from Virginia.

"Slowly," Muñoz said again. He spoke with an oily confidence that was at odds with his obsequiousness of only minutes before. He smiled. "I assure you, there are no crystal skulls to be had, at all. And this establishment never sold your friend's husband a serigraph of any type."

"Sorry," Dixon said. He looked embarrassed. "He must have signaled—"

"You will be very quiet now," Muñoz said. "All of you. Speak only when spoken to." He approached Sydney. "Who are you?" he asked.

"I *thought* you were a dealer in antiquities," she said.

"I know whom you work for," Muñoz said. He could have been an entirely different person now.

Even his body language had changed. This was no eager-to-please shopkeeper before her now, but someone accustomed to immediate and complete obedience. "I knew that American Intelligence would send someone."

It had all been a trap. Muñoz and his underlings had been waiting for her. How could they have failed so badly? How could she not have seen through his act? Alcatena had been dead even before her father had returned from Virginia. His killer had waited here only to see who would backtrack his work.

Muñoz shrugged. "You will talk now," he said. "Or you will talk later. Either way, it is of no great concern." He waved at his associates, and at the guns they held. "Do you know how these work?"

Sydney glared at him. "Not the specifics," she said.

Muñoz nodded. "Like a microwave oven, they boil water," he said. He half-smiled. "Did you know that the human body is more than ninety percent water?"

Even with adrenaline coursing through her, even with every sense functioning at peak efficiency, Sydney felt a chill of alarm. Muñoz's words, delivered so casually, explained just what had become of Alcatena's eyes.

Still watching her closely, Muñoz stepped to the bank of file servers and removed the jewelry ankh that clung to it. Metal and crystal crunched as he cast the disguised device to the floor and ground it beneath his foot. "My employer's secrets will remain his own," he said. "They would have, in any case. This place is not long for the world."

Now, he dipped one hand into his jacket pocket and drew out a small keypad. It held three buttons. Muñoz pressed one, waited five seconds, and then pressed a second. When he returned his full attention to Sydney, his thumb was resting squarely on the third.

"We spent some hours placing thermite charges at various points in the facility," he said. "Twelve of them. They respond to this switch."

"Covering your tracks?" Sydney asked. For whatever reason, the man was focusing on her. If she could continue to command his attention, it might give Dixon or Nadia a chance.

"Not my personal tracks, no," Muñoz said. He sounded studiously nonchalant.

"You can't detonate without killing us all," Sydney said.

"Without killing everyone who remains here," he corrected her, and moved back from Sydney. He waved his free hand at his subordinates. "Fernando, Raoul," he said. "Bring the two them over here," he said, and his underlings complied silently. In moments, Sydney, Nadia, and Dixon stood side by side, their backs to the wall. Muñoz's men backed away carefully.

"Move only as I tell you to," he said, his eyes still locked on Sydney. "Death by fire is painful. Death by disobedience would be far worse."

Sydney was watching him, too. There was no doubt that all three men were professionals, but Muñoz was enjoying himself just a little bit too much for his own good. She had dealt with men like him before, and recognized it easily now that his pose had fallen away. This was a man who liked power, but not the power that came with an empire or even as the leader of a team. This was a man who treasured the authority of having helpless people at his mercy.

Or, at least, people whom he thought were helpless.

"The restraints," Muñoz said. Still focused on Sydney, he had moved closer again.

Fernando's free hand dipped into his jacket pocket and withdrew three sets of handcuffs. Attempting to take some small measure of control over the situation, hoping for an opening, Sydney offered her wrists. If the gunman leaned close enough, she might have a chance to act. The man ignored her and presented the cuffs to Nadia, instead. Following Sydney's example, she reached for them.

"No. Secure yourself," Muñoz said. "No tricks." As Nadia complied, he continued. "Here is how we will proceed."

"I have a vehicle waiting outside. Once I am certain that we can do so safely, my men and I will escort you to it. You will move quietly, and without any attempt at escape." He indicated Alcatena's corpse. "My instructions were to reappropriate certain resources here, and then eliminate the proprietor without undue pain. That courtesy was not to extend to any who came looking for him."

Dixon accepted his cuffs from Raoul. At the very periphery of her vision, Sydney could see him make a show of fumbling with them, as if he did not know how to put them on. He, too, was stalling for time, hoping for an opportunity.

Muñoz saw it too. Angrily, he snapped, "No games!" For a split second, he looked away from Sydney.

Many things happened then. They happened very quickly and with surprising symmetry, as if the three APO agents had coordinated closely.

Nadia pulled her cuffed wrists close against her body. She surged forward in a savage head-butt that caught the chin of the man guarding her. Both grunted in pain from the impact. The gun her captor held flew from his grip, and then clattered onto the floor. Nadia's left foot came down hard on the man's right one, and the pain was enough to make him cry out. She punched him again, this time in the belly.

Sydney moved too. Her hands were still free, so she smashed one into Muñoz's nose with blinding speed, making cartilage crunch satisfactorily. In the same instant, her other hand darted out to grab his wrist. Her strong fingers ground down with crushing force on the nerve clusters there, momentarily paralyzing the muscles they controlled. Muñoz's fingers twitched ineffectually, trying to close but unable to. The button went un-pushed.

Raoul seemed stunned by the sudden activity to

his right and left. His gun hand swung as he tried to chose a target. Before he could decide, however, Dixon's big hand had closed on his smaller one and forced it back and up. He could still fire, but to no advantage.

"Dixon! Button!" Sydney barked. Muñoz was struggling against her. He was trying to free his trapped hand, or at least to take control of the detonator again, and it was all that Sydney could do to stop him. He squirmed in her grasp, throwing himself against her and then pulling back.

"Hands full," her partner snapped. His combatant had both hands on the microwave pistol now and was trying to wrest it free of Dixon's control. The two men struggled against each other.

Her hands still bound before her, Nadia had managed to knock her guard to the floor by slamming her entire body against him. She kneeled on Fernando's chest, pinning him with her weight. She brought her hands back and up now, then brought them down hard. The struggling man fell back, dazed. Clumsily, she began searching his pockets, looking for a key to her restraints. It was difficult work with both hands shackled together.

Muñoz was cursing, spitting Spanish words

that sounded hard and unpleasant. He had given up on freeing himself from Sydney's iron grip or regaining full control of the detonator. Instead, he lashed out at her, clawing for her eyes with hooked fingers. Instinctively, Sydney pulled back from the strike.

The movement was enough to loosen her grip. Muñoz twisted his arm, trying again to pull free. His left leg hooked her right one, and he tried to topple her. She fell against a workbench even as she kicked at him. Her free hand found the workbench's surface and groped for a weapon. It found a utility knife.

As Sydney stabbed at Muñoz, however, Raoul made his move. Rather than contend with Dixon any longer, he reached for Muñoz instead, groping for the detonator he held. A moment later, the keypad, like the gun before it, went flying. It spun crazily in midair and the fell to earth again, facedown.

"No!" Muñoz yelped.

The detonator struck the floor. It clicked as chance impact pushed the third button home.

"How long?" Sydney demanded. She knew that a countdown had started.

Muñoz didn't answer. Instead, he slithered out of Sydney's grip and threw himself to one side. Almost instantly, his hand closed on the microwave pistol that Fernando, Nadia's adversary, had lost.

"Back!" he snarled, scuttling backward on feet and one hand, moving like a crab. He kept the pistol trained in their direction. He moved clumsily, but his aim remained unerring as he struggled to his feet. To his men, he snarled, "Take her!"

He was pointing at Nadia. Immediately, his two henchmen flanked Sydney's still-cuffed sister. They half-escorted, half-dragged her back up the flight of stairs, but the work wasn't easy. The younger woman struggled desperately, kicking and clawing and biting even as Raoul's pistol dug into her side. As he edged through the door, the man who had identified himself as Muñoz paused.

"No one moves," he said.

The knife felt good in Sydney's hand. She had already found its balance. She judged the distance and the angle, more by intuition than with conscious thought. If she could just move fast enough—

"Drop it!" Muñoz ordered. "No one moves, none of you, or she dies before we reach the car."

The blade fell to the floor with a clatter, and Muñoz continued to back away from them.

He passed though the door and then was lost from view as the heavy barricade slid in its track. It slammed home with a sound like thunder.

Sydney raced up the stairs, Dixon close behind her. She pounded futilely on the heavy steel barrier that blocked her path. She cursed and spat, and shouted Nadia's name, too angry to think clearly. It seemed to her that she could hear a clock ticking.

"Syd!" Dixon said. He spoke with sanity and authority. "Syd! Get hold of yourself! This won't do any good!"

She pounded on the door some more, too terribly aware of the futility of it all.

Dixon clutched her shoulders. He shook her, hard enough to hurt, but pain was good. It cut through the near-panic she felt. "The passkey," he said urgently. "You got in, you can get us out!"

Of course. The electronic skeleton key was still in her kit. Sydney drew it out, slid it into the card reader, and took a deep breath. Their quarry easily could have deactivated the reader.

He hadn't. The door opened again. Darkness lay beyond. Muñoz and his people had shut down the gallery before joining her in the basement workshop.

Without waiting for their eyes to adjust, Sydney and Dixon sprinted though the gloom. More than once, she slammed into low display units, but she took no note of the pain. Behind them was death; somewhere ahead was her sister. Nothing else mattered.

How had it all gone so wrong? How could she have not seen that it was a trap?

Something in the shadowed gallery interrupted her headlong race. A toppled rack sent items that she could not see cascading in all directions. She ignored them. Ahead, she could see the night sky through window glass. The exit was ahead.

No time remained to fumble with a doorknob. Sydney used her forearms to shield her face and eyes, and dove headlong forward. Close behind her, Dixon did the same, and then they both lay sprawled on the sidewalk, amid broken glass and door frame. She heard tires squealing on cobblestones.

A moment later, the earth beneath her heaved as the workshop bombs exploded, and the world went away for a while.

CHAPTER 9

LOS ANGELES

As she concluded her report, Sydney felt as if she were before some exalted tribunal, and had just done a singularly poor job of presenting her case. It was absurd, she knew, but some corner of her mind would not relinquish the idea.

The room was quiet and still, but she knew that emotions ran high. Vaughn and Weiss both looked sympathetic. Marshall seemed quietly aghast, and Dixon had a stoic quality that spoke to his own role in the Peru assignment. Her father looked concerned, presumably as much about strategic issues as about her emotional well-being. All had watched and listened closely as she had presented the particulars of the field mission, weighing her words and actions.

She found her account wanting. How could they not?

If her fellow operatives were the jury, Arvin Sloane was the judge who presided over them. Only he had not looked directly at her as she delivered her report. Only Sloane had gazed aimlessly into the distance, his face an expressionless mask. He seemed to have aged ten years.

Sydney had briefed him personally before the meeting. A very difficult fifteen minutes had passed as she detailed how his daughter had been captured. The effect had been profound. His always-tired eyes now looked more tired still, and his typically reserved demeanor had given way to something colder, harder. Sydney had never seen him like this before. She had seen him mourn a loved one, and rage against defeat, but this was different. Sloane looked as if something inside him had shut down, or retreated behind heavy shields.

"Unfortunate," Sloane said. The single word seemed hopelessly inadequate to the task he had set it, and his voice was neutral and remote. "We can't allow ourselves to be in the business of providing captives for our enemies."

Sydney flinched. She thought of Nadia being dragged up the staircase. Her half sister had fought hard to avoid capture. It was up to Sydney and APO now to make sure that her fight had not been in vain.

It was strange. Sydney had worked very hard to inure herself against Sloane's habitual manipulation and deceit. In some ways, she had been successful in setting aside her emotions in order to make the current arrangement work, repugnant though it was. She had often wished never to see Arvin Sloane again, but now, she could not help but feel sympathy for his pain. Paradoxically, his refusal to show that pain made it all the more evident.

"We can get her back," Sydney said. The words felt bad in her mouth, and she knew that she sounded more defensive than she intended. "Muñoz wanted to take all three of us, and they wanted us alive. That means she's even more valuable to them now."

"We need to pursue this," Sloane said to all of

them, who had gathered together in the conference room. Now, at last, he glanced in Sydney's direction. "There were some developments during your absence. Marshall will explain."

Marshall stood. His dark eyes were troubled, and he looked in Sydney's direction for a long moment before commencing. She knew that he wanted to give her a kind word, or even a hug, but she also know that he knew better. These meetings were all business. Besides, she was in no frame of mind to accept anyone's pity.

"You did good, not getting shot," he finally said. "Those guns would have cooked you good, from the inside. That's what happened to Alcatena's eyes. Like eggs in a microwave. *Splurt!*" He made a noise like a wet explosion, incongruous but thoroughly evocative.

Marshall nodded in Jack Bristow's direction. "You were right before too," he said. "I did some research. Did you know that the Department of Defense tabled a microwave weapons initiative back in the 1970s?" His hands fidgeted as he spoke. "The official reason was humanitarian concerns, but the real one was, they couldn't make 'em work right. Effective range was short, and energy requirements were huge. No one could figure out how to make them practical." He pantomimed firing a pistol. "Someone has, now."

"Alcatena?" Sydney asked. She had to say something.

"No, not his bailiwick," Marshall said, shaking his head. "Or, not by himself. He's—he was a specialist. He made things small. Someone else solved the range problem, and increased usage efficiency. These things are really slick pieces of work."

As he spoke, he gradually became more animated, even enthusiastic. Marshall never seemed as thoroughly alive as he did when discussing a knotty technical problem. Even his typical nervousness dwindled as he explained the result of his studies of the captured gun. He spoke about waveform properties and polymerized superconductors, about x-ray transparent electronics and supersmall-scale microchips. After a minute or so, when most of his audience had begun to glaze over, a throat-clearing cough from Sloane brought the technical expert in him back to Earth.

"Sorry," Marshall said. His shoulders moved up and then down again, and he looked momentarily sheepish. "I get carried away."

"Just summarize," Sloane said, his voice dead.

"Okay, okay," Marshall said. He took a deep breath. "Now that the heavy lifting's done, these are probably pretty cheap to mass-produce. They're just power cells and waveform generators, and a CPU. Very nice, very compact, but pretty standard stuff." He paused. "Except for the firmware. The firmware is special."

Sloane didn't seem to be paying much attention, Sydney noticed. Perhaps Marshall had briefed him in advance, as she had. Perhaps he simply had other things on his mind.

Marshall continued. "That's what makes them work." He groped for an explanation. "It's like—like your computer. With the operating system installed, it's a wonderful thing—a tool, a toy, a friend." He blushed faintly. "Wipe the OS, and all you have is a paperweight."

His right hand still mimed gripping a pistol. He pointed the phantom gun at Jack Bristow for emphasis, then realized his faux pas. It was never wise to point a gun at Jack Bristow, not even an imaginary one. His fingers snapped open, and he continued his report hastily. "Uh, sorry," he said. "But the sample you found, it's been wiped. It wiped itself. I was able to reverse-engineer some of the code and figure out the gizmo's basics, but the main code lines are gone and I can't recover them."

"I didn't do anything to it," Jack said. His words were a simple statement of fact.

Marshall shook his head again. "I think it wiped itself," he repeated. "I think it was set to dump its code, after a single discharge."

The elder Bristow looked at him blankly.

"As a demonstration," Marshall said. "To show what it could do. The first shot was free."

"Good thing you aimed it at a wall," Eric Weiss said very softly, but not softly enough. He went silent again as Jack glared at him.

Marshall continued. "It's, like, you can download a movie, pay for a week, but, you know, you don't get around to watching it. The wife wants to go dancing, the baby's too much fun to play with, so you don't get around to your movie for eight days." He paused. "Phht! Gone! It's wiped itself off your drive. Don't you just hate it when that happens?"

No one answered.

"I think that's what your gun's software did," he said.

"Why would anyone do something like that?" Jack prodded. "What are the advantages?"

"It gives the manufacturer vastly greater control over the end-use of his wares," Sloane said. He looked thoughtful. "He can equip an army and then demand additional payment if his customer wants the weapons to keep working."

Marshall nodded. "Freshness-dated firepower," he said. "Maybe even by remote control."

Sloane continued. "Alternatively, he can change customers in mid-conflict," he said. He was warming to the subject. Clearly, it appealed to his thought processes. "Whichever side in a conflict is willing to pay more, gets the capability. Gets it and keeps it."

Marshall nodded again. "There's more," he said. "Upgrades. The hardware is a platform for the software. The same hardware grows new features when you swap out the programming code." He mimed holding a gun again. "Improve the firmware, get new capabilities. Longer range, maybe, or greater signal throughput. Anything the hardware can support."

Something like horror gnawed at Sydney. Each possibility that Sloane or Marshall raised suggested more. "That would be a . . . a paradigm shift," she said slowly. "An entirely new approach to small-arms equipage."

"Small?" Marshall asked. "There's no reason you couldn't use the same principle in a fieldpiece." He held his hands before them and moved them apart, his outstretched arms indicating a weapon of considerable size. "And you haven't seen small yet," he said. His hands moved close together. "The only real limit is the size of the power cells."

"Who came up with these things?" Vaughn asked. Like Sydney, he sounded more than slightly aghast. "Not Alcatena?"

"No, no," Marshall said. "Like I said, he's—he was a specialist. The underlying technology—"

Sloane interrupted. "Marshall," he said, coolly but still engaged. "Does the name 'Burton Hildebrandt' mean anything in this context?"

Marshall fell silent, and his eyes narrowed. Sydney could almost see the gears shifting inside his head. In casual conversation he could be mercurial, even scattershot, in his remarks, but once he had focused on a technical topic, he was not easily diverted. Sloane's question had come as a surprise, and one that he needed a moment to process.

"German," he finally said. "Radiation physicist. Did a lot of work for the old Eastern Bloc. I've read some of his papers. This could be his."

"Hildebrandt is dead," Sloane said, with absolute certainty. "But this could be the product of his organization."

"Dead?" Jack Bristow asked. "Are we sure?"

"Dead," Sloane said. He sounded absolutely certain, and Sydney wondered why.

Marshall tugged nervously at the lobe of one ear. "It could be," he said again. He raised one hand palm down and rocked it from side to side in the universal sign language for uncertainty. "He sure is—was—smart enough," he said. He looked at Jack. "You know who Nikola Tesla was, don't you?"

"No," Jack said.

"Early twentieth-century inventor," Weiss interjected smoothly. "He was a contemporary of Edison and Houdini, friend of Mark Twain. Big believer in wireless transmission of electricity. Claimed he could revolutionize warfare. He had a lab on Long Island and threw lightning bolts all over the place." He grinned slightly. "Long Island was pretty different in those days."

"Hildebrandt did stuff like that, only with

microwaves," Marshall said. "Probably terrible for TV reception." He looked to Sloane again. "But he's dead?"

Sloane nodded. He gestured in Weiss's direction. "Follow up on this," he said. "See what you can find out about any successors."

Weiss nodded.

It was Vaughn's turn now. At Sloane's prompting, he stood to deliver his report. For a split second, his eyes locked with Sydney's, and then slid away. Something about the way he looked at her said that he had no good news to tell.

"I've tried most standard channels, but no luck. No one in the Intelligence community wants to talk to us about Alcatena, or about Muñoz and where he might be now," he said. "South American assets in general and Peruvian resources in particular are being unusually uncooperative. Even for them." He took a deep breath. "Either they still regard Alcatena as one of their own, or they're expecting their own delivery of microwave pistols."

His words carried ominous implications. Peru was a major supplier to the world drug trade, and its mountainous reaches were a hotbed of revolutionary activity. Introducing weapons as discreet and advanced as the little pistol into that arena would have dramatic effects. It could easily destabilize the entire region.

Making them available in the United States would be even worse.

":I hope not. You're working the issue?" Sloane asked. It was more of a statement than a question.

"Eric and I are," Vaughn said as Weiss inclined his head slightly in acknowledgment. "The local law-enforcement personnel should be a bit more cooperative." He looked at his watch. "I leave for Peru in an hour," he continued. "I know some people down there who know the value of a dollar—or lots of dollars."

"I'll go with you," Sydney said eagerly.

"No," Sloane said. "I want you here, working with Eric."

"Hey!" Weiss interjected sharply. Clearly, he was at least as worried about Nadia as Sydney was, even if for different reasons. "I want in on this too!"

Sloane shook his head again. "I want both of you here," he said.

"But I've been there," she objected. "I can—"

"I want you here with Eric," Sloane said again, and now he was the old Sloane again, delivering orders that commanded full obedience. He looked around the table, directing his gaze at each operative in turn. Sydney was last, and his eyes locked with hers for a long moment before he continued. "Be ready to reconvene at a moment's notice," he said.

"We'll get her back," Sydney said.

Sloane looked at her. "I appreciate everyone's concern," he said. "But we can't act until we get more information. And our first priority has to be the professional one. We have to find out who is behind this."

"I won't be benched," Sydney told Sloane, ten minutes later. "I will not be put on the sidelines."

She stood before Sloane's spotless desk. He sat behind it, leaning back in his chair with his chin resting in one hand. He faced her with the total confidence of a tiger in his lair, secure in absolute power.

Most of Sydney's sympathy was gone now, or at least driven to the back of her mind for the moment. Sloane's order that she work with Weiss rather than Vaughn had done that. The offhand directive had felt like condemnation.

"I'm the one who makes the assignments, Sydney," Sloane said. He looked at her levelly. "I appreciate your concern and I know that you're anxious to help, but your skills are needed here."

"Weiss doesn't need me. Vaughn might," she said sharply. "I have field experience in Peru."

"Gained most recently when Nadia was captured," Sloane said. "I need a fresh perspective."

She stared at him. "You want to bench me for that?" she asked. "She's my sister—"

"Half sister," Sloane corrected, still coolly. Sometimes, he could be a stickler for detail.

"My sister and my friend," Sydney continued. "We've got to get her back."

"Nadia is my daughter, Sydney," Sloane said. Now, at last, there was some real emotion in his voice. "Does that make her as important to me as she is to you? Or less? Tell me, please."

She blinked, stunned. The question was unfair and had no answer. She half-hated herself for making him ask it, but could not deny that he had the right.

"Tell me," Sloane prodded.

"I'm sorry," she said. The words tasted like ashes.

He said nothing.

"But you can't bench me," she said, half-pleading. "I want to be part of this. I need to be."

"You will be," Sloane said. "Sydney, you're one

of the best in the world at what you do. You're one of APO's greatest assets. Do you truly think that I would fail to include you on an effort as important as this one? You think that I would forego Nadia's best chance at coming home alive?"

The veiled accusation took her aback. Without realizing it, she had been standing at rigid attention. That ended now. The long muscles of her back and neck began to relax, and the pounding of her heart slowed. "No," she said softly. "No. You're too practical for that." The compliment was grudging but sincere.

"Good," Sloane said. "But I am concerned. About you."

"About me?" she asked. Her remaining anger gave way to confusion.

Sloane leaned forward. He rested his hands on the desktop and looked at her, a look of earnest empathy in his eyes. "What is it that troubles you, Sydney?" he asked.

"Nadia," Sydney said. She didn't like admitting weakness, especially to Sloane, but there was no denying the truth. "I'm worried about her."

"No," he said. He shook his head. "Not Nadia. I've known you since you were very young, Sydney.

There was a time when you visited my home regularly. I like to think I know you well."

That was true. The accuracy of his observation galled, but it could not be denied. There had been months and even years when Sloane had seemed closer to her than her own flesh and blood. That he had preyed upon that closeness and destroyed it didn't mean that it had never existed. In many ways, Sloane knew her better than she knew him.

"Something weighs on your mind," he continued. "You haven't been sleeping well. I can see that."

"I'm fine," she said, defensive again. His concern repelled her. "Don't worry about me."

"You want to be part of the rescue effort," Sloane said. "I want you to be part of it. But are you certain that you can perform?"

"Don't question my operational readiness," Sydney said, more sharply still.

"I've reviewed your range scores," he said implacably. "You're still the best we have, but you're not as good as you were even two weeks ago. I ask you again: What is it that troubles you?"

"Nothing," she said, but the words sounded hollow. She wondered how he had gotten the information. "That was an off day, that's all."

"You're very important to me, Sydney," Sloane said. "I told you more than once that letting the two of us be put in opposition is one of the great regrets of my life."

"You made that choice," Sydney said. Sloane's track through her life was long and tangled, with many detours and wrong turns along the way. He had been many things to her: family friend and mentor, supervisor and nemesis. Each time she had found a category for him, he had confounded her by revealing some new agenda or ulterior motive. Even though they now worked together once more, she knew that she would never truly trust him again. "You made it many times," she said.

"Yes," he said in simple agreement, and with sadness. Oddly, Sydney had no doubt that his remorse, at least, was sincere. He continued. "Something is troubling you, and it's affecting your performance. Take the time to resolve it, I beg you."

"I'm fine," she told him again. "All that I need to resolve is Nadia's situation."

He shook his head. "I'm worried about her, too, Sydney," he said. "But I'm worried about you both. I couldn't bear to lose you."

As Sydney left Sloane's office, a thought occurred to her. It bubbled up from her subconscious, absurd at first but insistent.

It was Nadia who had been captured. It was Sloane's own daughter who was in enemy hands, her status unknown. Despite that, the APO director had insisted on addressing and discussing Sydney's well-being.

Sloane had voiced more concern about her than he had about his flesh and blood. He knew something that he wasn't sharing.

Sloane felt more than heard the presence at the doorway. He had been studying the screen of his computer and, before looking up to receive his new visitor, he tapped a key and the screen went blank. He swiveled in his chair as Jack Bristow entered his office. The door clicked shut behind him as he settled, without invitation, into the guest chair.

Sydney had stood to make her demands; Jack sat. That was the difference between angry confrontation and easy pragmatism.

"Hello, Jack," Sloane said.

"You know something," Jack said. He offered no greeting or preamble.

"This seems to be my day for closed-door sessions with your family," Sloane said.

"I paid attention during the briefing," Jack said, undeterred. He spoke with the tenacity and forthrightness that Sloane had always regarded as being among his best traits. "You're good at hiding things. Good, but not perfect, and I've known you for a long time, Arvin. You know more about Hildebrandt than you're telling."

"We work on a need-to-know basis, Jack," Sloane reminded him. It was a guiding principle that informed all APO operations. "You know that."

The elder Bristow seemed utterly relaxed, but Sloane knew better than to judge him by surface demeanor. Jack Bristow was a dangerous man, and always would be. Not unlike a jungle cat, even when at rest, he was ready to strike.

"I just got off the phone with some contacts at Interpol," Jack said. "The dates line up. This Hildebrandt met his end while you were rogue. Tell me, Arvin, did you have a hand in that?"

"Our paths crossed, briefly," Sloane said. "I can't say that we were friends."

"Competitors, then?" Jack asked. Not so long ago, the United States Intelligence community had

159

been locked in a competition to secure the esoteric technologies left behind by Carlos Rimbaldi. Sloane had been a member of the opposition, and he had not been alone.

"He was no competition either," Sloane said. Despite the tense situation, he permitted himself a faint smile. He had many adversaries, but little real competition. "But he's dead now. I'm certain of that."

"You've been wrong before," Jack said, but didn't press the issue. Instead, he asked, "What did Sydney want?"

Ordinarily he would have declined to answer, but the time, the circumstances, seemed to warrant a response. "To accompany Vaughn to Peru," Sloane said. "She thinks her current assignment is not the best use of her capabilities."

"She's right. Weiss doesn't need any help," Jack said.

"Perhaps not," Sloane replied. "But the assignment wasn't for his benefit."

Jack's eyes flashed slightly at his words. "You can't blame her for what happened in Cuzco," he said.

"I don't. I believe that she does, however."

"Muñoz and his men were waiting for our team," Jack continued.

"They were waiting for someone," Sloane corrected him.

The familiar bulldog tenacity reasserted itself. "For someone, then," Jack said. "If you're trying to protect Sydney, or if you don't feel you can trust her in this—"

Sloane interrupted. "Tell me, Jack," he said. "In all our years together, have you ever known me to hesitate to do anything, to make any sacrifice that I judged necessary? Ever?"

The other man sighed. "No. No, I haven't." Jack paused for a deep breath. "That's not a compliment."

"And as for my not trusting Sydney, quite the contrary," Sloane continued. "It's she who doubts me. Understandable, I suppose. Our pasts tend to come back to haunt us."

SOMEWHERE

The world returned, but only slowly. First came light, making its presence known even through closed eyelids. Following it was a sour, metallic taste that filled her mouth. Then Nadia Santos could hear her own heart's sluggish beat.

She opened her eyes and immediately wished she hadn't. The fluorescent glare stabbed at her from above. She blinked her stinging eyes several times, but it didn't seem to help. For some reason, her vision was slower to adjust than it should have been. Her surroundings were soft-edged and blurry, and she could feel the crustiness of long sleep at the corners of her eyes.

She had been asleep, and for a long time, from the way she felt. How long?

"Do not try to move," someone said, to her left. The words were perfectly pronounced, but the voice had a muffled quality.

Nadia ignored the command, but only with effort. Her muscles felt like lead, and they seemed to work against her as she turned to see who had spoken. A man in surgical whites stood at her bedside. His eyes were gray and solemn, and they peered at her from above a surgical mask. One of the man's hands held a hypodermic needle. The other held an ampoule.

Nadia became aware of soreness in her shoulder. He had injected something into her.

"Let the stimulant do its work," the man said. With a grunt of effort, he raised the bed's side-rail and locked it into place. The metal bars of the rail were brightly polished, and their sheen made Nadia's eyes hurt some more. "You have slept for several days."

Images filled Nadia's mind. She remembered the showdown in Cuzco, and remembered being pushed, kicking and screaming, into a waiting limousine. She remembered an arrogant Hispanic man leaning close to clamp a gas mask onto her face, and she remembered darkness had followed.

"Who are you?" she demanded. Her tongue and lips were nearly numb and each word was a struggle, but her thoughts came more clearly now. She recognized what she felt as the symptoms of deep anesthesia. "Where . . . where am I?"

"Questions for another time," the man said. "When you have awakened completely, attendants will feed and bathe you. Do not attempt to trouble them; they are well-trained."

He was not speaking in his native tongue, Nadia realized. The cadence was wrong. He spoke English without an accent, but his phrasing had a stilted quality. It was the kind of phrasing characteristic of a speaker's second or third language, especially one learned in adulthood. She filed the bit of information away in her mind. It could be useful.

He continued. "You are a rare prize," he said. "I knew that Sloane would send someone to investigate my operations. I had not expected his daughter."

Shaking her head made Nadia's eyes hurt more, and made the world swim crazily. "No," she said. "Don't know who—"

"Do not deny it," her host said. He moved to the foot of her bed and set the hypo and ampoule on a small table there. He occupied much of her field of vision now, resting gloved hands on the bed frame as he gazed down at her. Behind him was an open door, and Nadia could see a white corridor beyond that. As she watched him she saw a wheeled gurney roll by, guided by another figure in medical robes. Reflexively, her eyes tracked the cart's passage. Some of the man's earlier words made more sense now.

He noticed her change in expression, and nodded. "You are a guest in my clinic," he said. "It was a simple matter to sample and verify your DNA."

Nadia tried to move her hands, but could not. The muscles obeyed her commands, but to no good effect. Soft restraints held her arms and legs immobile. She was anchored to the hospital bed's rails and they were solid, resisting. "Verified against what?" she asked.

The mask hid most of his face, but not his eyes. They sparkled now, and the skin surrounding them wrinkled. He was smiling. "Against samples previously taken," he said.

Comprehension dawned, and with it, concern. To identify her as the child of Arvin Sloane, he must have had a sample of her father's genetic material on hand for comparison.

Her captor was part of her father's world.

"But I must wonder," the man continued. "What kind of man would involve his daughter in such business?"

"My choice too," she said.

He nodded in acknowledgment. "Perhaps," he said. "But he is adept at guiding others into choices he wants them to make."

There was nothing to say to that. Nadia had met her father only comparatively recently, and he was still something of a stranger to her. Sydney had told her tales, and her own research had disclosed other troubling accounts, but neither comported

165

very well with the graying, reserved man she was slowly coming to know.

"But we can talk of that another time," the man continued. "We will have many evenings together, you and I."

"No," she said. "Someone will come after me." The words were a bluff, but all that she could think of to say. There seemed no way for Sloane or the others to know where she was.

"Perhaps," he said. "But I believe your father values your safety too greatly for that."

"He's not a man who goes away," Nadia said.

"He would do well to consider doing so," her host said. "I have no wish to contend with him now. I had sought to retire from his arena, to wash my hands of Rimbaldi and the Covenant and all the rest and pursue new endeavors. To find him involving himself in my enterprises again . . ."

His words trailed off, and he shrugged. "The consequences are on his head, then," he concluded. "And yours."

CHAPTER 10

LOS ANGELES

Jack Bristow sipped espresso. The thick coffee was hot and strong, brewed from fresh-ground premium beans, and he allowed himself a moment to savor it. The bone-white cup, scarcely larger than a shot glass, clinked as he returned it to the matching saucer. Under other circumstances, he might have placed it more carefully, to avoid generating the telltale sound, but not today, not now. He was alone.

The day was nearing its end. Outside, the sun had dropped low enough in the cloudless sky to grow and gain a reddish hue, and the angled rays it cast through louvered blinds cast shadowed strips on the breakfast nook's wall. Through those same windows he could hear birds sing territorial warnings to their neighbors as they prepared to bed down for the night. It would be dark soon, but Jack didn't mind. The night held no terrors for him.

He was in an apartment, small but neatly furnished. He had seated himself so that he could face the place's entrance, and so that the table was between himself and the door. On the table, beside his cup and saucer, was the automatic pistol that was today's weapon of choice. Next to that was a folded newspaper.

He had lifted the cup for another taste of coffee when he heard what he had been waiting for. A lock rattled as a key turned in it, and a deadbolt slid back. Jack set the cup back down, silently this time, and moved his hand closer to the gun.

The door opened. Michael Vaughn stood framed in the opening. One hand held his keys and a grocery bag. The other hand, his gun hand, was free, and it darted inside his windbreaker as he saw that he had a visitor. Jack knew that he wore a concealed shoulder holster.

"Welcome back," Jack said. As he saw Vaughn's hand retreat from the weapon, he allowed his own to do the same.

"It was just a quick hop. Peru and back. I hope you haven't been waiting long," Vaughn said with slight sarcasm.

"We need to talk, and I didn't want to do it at the office."

"How did you get in here?" Vaughn asked. He sounded only mildly surprised as he closed the door behind himself. "Without my knowing it, I mean."

"I've been in the business longer than you have," Jack said. He drank more coffee. "I've been here an hour."

"I had some shopping to do," Vaughn said. He set his bag on the kitchen counter and pulled out three cans, a bottle of milk, and another, smaller bag made of white paper. The cans went in the cupboard and the milk he put in the refrigerator, where it sat nearly alone. He raised the paper bag and looked quizzically at Jack. "Biscotti?" he asked, offering. "These were for breakfast, but since you've helped yourself to the espresso already, you're welcome to one."

Jack shook his head. "We need to talk," he said again.

Before answering, Vaughn opened another cupboard. He took out a cup-and-saucer set that matched the one Jack was using, and another, slightly larger plate. He put two of the hard-baked cookies on the plate and served himself from the already-primed espresso machine. Jack let the entire domestic ritual pass without comment or interruption. He understood the reason for it. As surely as the birds outside were, Vaughn was marking his territory. He did it with a show of confidence and strength rather than with song, but the intent was the same. Vaughn was demonstrating that finding an armed visitor waiting for him in his own home had not unnerved him.

Vaughn seated himself at his own table, opposite Jack. He pantomimed another offer of biscotti, and got another refusal. He nodded and said, "So talk."

"It's about Sydney," Jack said. The words were familiar.

Vaughn nodded again. He broke one of the cookies and dunked it in his cup. "Big surprise," he said, then bit and chewed.

It always seemed to be about Sydney.

170

Vaughn swallowed and continued. "Why the hardware, then?" he asked.

The gun was heavy and cool in Jack's hand as he returned it to the holster that he wore under his suit coat. "I got in," he said. "Someone else could have. I don't like surprises."

"You don't like being surprised," Vaughn corrected. "I asked before. How'd you get in undetected?"

"You've got a hole in your security," Jack said. "I'm sure, now that you know it's there, you can find it yourself."

"Okay," Vaughn said, nonplussed. He ate more biscotti and drank espresso. "Sydney, then," he continued. "You know we're not exactly an item these days. Not in the active sense, at least."

"She still listens to you," Jack said. He was thoroughly versed in the history of the entanglements between his daughter and the other CIA operative. "I know how you feel—how you still feel about each other." He paused, choosing his words carefully. "I don't entirely approve of that, but I have more respect for Sydney's judgment than she seems to think."

It was a compliment.

"I can understand that," Vaughn said. "But I hope that's not what you wanted to talk about."

"No," Jack said. He shook his head, but only slightly. "About what happened in Cuzco."

Now, at last, Vaughn looked irritated. "This isn't appropriate," he said. "It's not the time or the place. And she did a good job."

"A good job," Jack said in agreement. "Not a great one. And I think we're both accustomed to greatness from Sydney."

"Go ahead," Vaughn said grudgingly. He had finished the first biscotti and was halfway though the second. This time, as he chewed, the aroma of hazelnut scented the air.

"She let someone get the drop on her," Jack said. "She almost didn't get out of the basement, even though she had the key."

"Someone got the drop on Dixon and Nadia, too," Vaughn pointed out. "You're not here about them."

"They're not Sydney," Jack said. It was the only explanation he felt any need to offer. "They're both good—even great—but they don't perform to her standard. You know that, and I know that."

"Yes," Vaughn said reluctantly. "I've noticed

some issues myself. Her marksmanship is off, for one thing."

"Oh?" Jack prompted. He knew the details, but also knew that Vaughn would be more likely to cooperate if he contributed as well.

In succinct sentences, Vaughn summarized the shooting-range session with Sydney and Nadia, and the high scores that hadn't been quite as high as they should have been. "Something is definitely wrong," he said.

"I'm glad you agree," Jack said. He indicated the newspaper that had lain on the table between them all this time. It was an issue of the *Washington Post.* He had gone to the minor inconvenience of securing the actual paper rather than download and print its contents. Computer transactions left trails that a handful of change at a newsstand did not. "Page B-16," Jack said.

Newspaper rustled as it unfolded. Vaughn found the right page and folded the others back so that he could read it more easily. Midway down B-16 was a block of text topped by a 20-point headline. "'Friends Rally Around Shooting Victim,'" Vaughn read aloud. He looked at Jack. "Still this?" he asked.

Jack nodded. "That's why we need to talk," he said. "She's hurting."

"She took a bullet," Vaughn said.

"Not the Wyatt woman," Jack said. "Sydney. This is just the kind of thing that hits her where she lives."

"I know," Vaughn replied. He toyed with his espresso cup. "Sometimes I think she cares too much."

"I think that at times, too," Jack said. "But I think it's because she cares so much that she's such a great agent. Physical skill, reaction time, dedication—all those are important, but it's her heart that gives her the edge."

"But now the edge is cutting her," Vaughn said slowly.

Jack nodded.

"You should be talking to her," Vaughn said.

"No," Jack said. He kept the sadness he felt from his voice as he continued. "She won't listen to me. She might listen to you."

The talk-show host, smirking to reveal the gap between his incisors, said something that was absurd, cryptic, and nearly nonsensical. His sidekick, a bald-headed bandleader who had elfin features and wore dark glasses, said something even sillier. Both men laughed, and more laughter welled up obediently from the studio audience.

Alone in her thoughts, Sydney scarcely noticed. She was half-sitting, half-lying on the couch in her living room. She wore a long nightgown, practical but not stifling, and she had drawn her legs up beneath her for warmth. Her feet were bare. The television was on less to entertain or engage than to provide background noise, and the illusion of companionship. She had deliberately selected something that would satisfy those criteria. The choice had taken more thought than it should have.

Her left hand held a pint of designer-brand coffee ice cream, high quality but higher priced. Her right held a silver teaspoon. As the gap-toothed man continued his discourse, she ferried a quarter-spoon load of frigid milk, cream, sugar, and natural flavors to her mouth.

There was a theory about ice cream. When Sydney had been in college, she had heard it discussed many times by other girls of her acquaintance, mostly as a joke. No one had really believed the theory, but even Sydney had found herself acting as if she did. Supposedly, one could eat even very large quantities of fattening foods without gaining weight if one did so in minute increments. She had run informal experiments countless times over the years, to prove or disprove the hypothesis, but without definitive results.

Tonight had seemed to be a good time to try again. The confection was thick and rich and carried at least the illusion of nourishment. Most of all, it was comfort food, a reminder of happier times.

The phone rang, startling her. She stabbed the spoon into the nearly empty container and left it there, then reached for the phone. This was her commercial landline phone, the number that her friends used. She couldn't imagine which of them would call this late, or that they would for any reason other than an emergency. "Yes?" she said into the receiver.

"I'd like to order a pizza," a familiar voice said.

Despite herself, she laughed. "My God, I have got to get this number changed," she said. "When did you get back?"

When Sydney had first worked for the CIA and pretended to still work for SD-6, Vaughn had been her Agency handler and a "wrong number" call for pizza had been the code signal to meet with him.

"A few hours ago," he said.

"Did you learn anything?" she asked urgently.

"A little. Nothing major. But that's not why I called. Look, I want to talk to you about some stuff, and I want to do it before the meeting tomorrow. You're still up, right?"

"Um," Sydney said. She pulled the robe closer around herself. "If it's an emergency—"

"Scratch that question," Vaughn said. "I know you're still up."

She didn't bother to ask how. "I'm up," she said. She paused. "I could use some company, actually. How soon?"

"How fast can you make it to the front door?" Vaughn asked.

Sydney held the receiver in one hand for a long moment and stared at it silently. She shook her head and rolled her eyes, then returned it to its cradle. She didn't speak again until she had opened the door to reveal Michael Vaughn standing on her doorstep.

He looked good. He looked more than good; he looked welcome. He wore black chinos, and a black collarless shirt beneath a gray sports jacket. He grinned at her, tucking his wireless phone into the jacket pocket with his right hand. On his left he balanced a small box, square and shallow and aromatic. Hooked in the fingers of the same hand was a small plastic grocery bag.

"Hey," he said, and handed her the pizza.

"Hey, yourself," she said. She paused again. "I thought we were taking things slow. You look like you're on a booty call."

He shook his head, and his grin evaporated. "Just here to talk," he said as he stepped inside. "Talk, and eat. I thought you might like a snack."

"Well, my good friends Häagen and Dazs have already helped me with that," she said, but he was already in the kitchen, busily pulling plates from the cupboard. She went to the living room and reclaimed the ice cream, replaced its top, and put the pint back in the freezer, where it belonged. "But pizza's not such a bad idea."

He nodded. "Good, because I'm starving," he said, and handed her a plate with two slices. "Here. Feta and spinach," he continued, taking a matching pair for himself. "I've got wine coolers," he said. When she shook her head, he took one and put the other in the refrigerator.

Almost anyone else, Sydney would have thought at least slightly presumptuous for making himself so much at home, but Vaughn was a special case. His role in her life was at least as complex as anyone else's role in her life, but it had been almost entirely a positive, enjoyable thing. Even when they had been at loggerheads over operational or emotional issues, the underlying mutual respect and affection had remained. She could get mad at him, but not for something as trivial as showing up on her doorstep after midnight.

A moment later, they were seated together on the couch, close but not too close. The pizza box sat on the low coffee table between them and the television, with a stack of napkins beside it.

"Who's on tonight?" he asked, pointing at the television.

"I don't know," she said as she thumbed the remote's mute button. "I don't care. Driveshaft was on earlier."

"Driveshaft?" he said, and smiled. It was one of Sydney's favorite bands. "They're great."

She was too busy eating to agree. She found that she was hungrier than she had thought, and hungry for real food. She demolished the entire first slice before she asked him, "Okay. What's up?"

"Well, you are, for starters," he said. He sipped his drink. "Why?"

"Why?"

"I'm all jet-lagged. What's your excuse?" he asked. "Can't sleep?"

"I can sleep," she said, honestly enough. There was no need to tell him how poorly. Better to make it a joke. "I can sleep anytime I want to, I'll have you know."

"Your eyes are tired," Vaughn said, with disarming frankness. He leaned close and pushed back a stray hair.

Rather than respond, she took another bite of pizza. It was good, substantial stuff and it seemed to fill a hole in her that the ice cream had missed.

"We have to talk, Syd," Vaughn said. "People are worried about you."

"You've been talking with Sloane," she said sharply.

He shook his head. "No."

"Who, then?" she asked, still sharply.

"Me, for starters," he said. "I'm worried about you."

"And I'm worried about Nadia," she said. "It's been days now."

Vaughn sighed. He shook his head again, but said nothing as he helped himself to another slice of pizza. Two bites and a sip later, he continued. "No," he said. "It's not Nadia. It's not Peru—or not entirely. Remember the day at the range?"

A target silhouette filled Sydney's mind's eye. It was black and red on white, with holes that let the light through. Not all of the holes were where she had intended them to be. "Those were perfectly acceptable scores," she said. Suddenly, the pizza didn't taste so good. Rather than meet his gaze, she got up and went to the kitchen. As she filled a glass with soda water, she called back to him, "And everyone has an off day."

"Not you," he said. "Not that off."

His words were a surprise. "I'm supposed to be Wonder Woman now?" she asked sourly.

She sat herself more closely to him this time, without conscious thought. Vaughn had been many things to her during the years that she had known him. He had been her contact and handler, her partner and comrade in arms, her lover and friend. If the events of the past few years had led them to take things slow for a while, the deep bond of intimacy had lost none of its strength. It felt good to sit so close to someone who loomed so large in her life, no matter what the topic of discussion.

"When I was prepping for Peru, I had a chat with Nadia," Vaughn continued. Sydney winced as he said the name. "She said you'd been having bad dreams."

"Just the one," Sydney said. She saw no point in telling him that she'd had the dream more than once.

Implacably, he continued. "I've noticed you looking tired," he said. "If you're sleeping, it's not well." He took a deep breath. "I spoke with Dixon a few hours ago."

Now, she felt genuine anger well up inside her. "Investigating me?" she said sharply. It was one thing for Vaughn to pick up on idle comments and gossip, or on his own observations. It was quite another to go looking for dirt.

"No," he said. "Just trying to help a friend."

"Maybe," she said. "Maybe the friend doesn't need the help." She spoke slowly and with great reluctance.

"I don't believe that," Vaughn said. He set the remnants of his meal aside and took one of her hands in both of his. She did not pull back. "I don't think you do either."

She said nothing.

"The incident in D.C.—"

"That building was supposed to be empty," Sydney said. The vehemence of her own words surprised her.

"It wasn't, Syd. A lot of things aren't the way they're supposed to be," Vaughn said. "You have to know that."

His patience was just a little bit too obvious. Sydney pulled her hand from his. All the frustration and fatigue she had felt for days coalesced. "Gee," she said, "do you think so!?"

"No," Vaughn said. Still patient, he drained the last of his drink and gazed at her. There was no challenge or judgment in his voice or in his eyes as he continued, only compassion. "I think you're stuck."

That drew her up short. "Stuck?" she said.

"Yes, stuck," he said. "I think what happened in D.C. affected you more deeply than you realize and you can't get past it."

"You're talking PTSD," Sydney said. "Post-traumatic stress disorder. I didn't know you were a shrink now too."

"I'm not, and I'm not," he said. "But I think I know part of what's wrong." He pulled a folded slip of paper from his jacket pocket as he spoke. "Dixon's not the only one I spoke with, Syd. I bent a few rules and asked Marshall to do me a favor, off the clock and on his home system."

Sydney drank her soda water but said nothing. She had no idea what he was talking about. "You were right earlier," she said. The conversation was wandering, and she had no idea where it was going. "I'm tired. If this can wait—"

He shook his head, still with infinite patience. "Marshall's been fooling around with facial modeling and manipulation software," he said. "I asked him to run an image for me."

He handed Sydney the paper without further comment. She unfolded it and blinked in surprise. "Oh," Sydney said. "Oh, my God."

Marshall's fax presented a pair of images. One was of a woman she recognized with sorrow and regret so intense that she nearly wept. The other, according to the note below it, was a projection of the same woman, as she might look some ten years later.

Both were of Francie Califo, dead and gone for more than two years now. The second might also have been a picture of Keisha Wyatt, the woman who had been wounded in Washington. The hairstyle and skin tone were different, but the shape of the eyes and the jawline angles matched exactly. Now that the resemblance had been demonstrated, Sydney wondered how she ever could have missed it. "I should have seen it," she said.

"You did," Vaughn told her. "Part of you did. You were high on adrenaline and someone was trying to kill you. Your conscious mind was too busy to see, but part of you did."

"And that's why I'm stuck," Sydney said in a dead voice. She thought about her sub-par shooting score and about the anger she had felt when Vaughn had called her on it. She thought about Peru and Nadia. "That's what I can't get past."

He had her hand again, and he nodded. He spoke with low urgency, saying, "You can get past it, Sydney. You have to."

Tears were spilling from her eyes now. Vaughn dabbed at them with a pizza napkin, but she waved him away. "No," she said. "No, I can handle it." Despite herself, she laughed softly. When Vaughn looked at her quizzically, she said, "That explains the ice cream."

"Huh?" he asked.

She blinked her eyes some more and then wiped at the tears with her bare hand. "That's how I ID-ed the duplicate," she said. "I offered her coffee ice cream. The real Francie didn't like it." Again, she laughed. "So," she said. "What now?"

"You get past it," Vaughn said. "If you need help, you get help. But either way, you get past it."

She nodded in agreement. "But how?" she asked softly.

"By not hiding from it."

CHAPTER 11

LOS ANGELES

It was a wonderful day, the kind of day that Marshall liked best. God was in his Heaven and all was right with the world. His baby had slept through the night, and his wife had worked with him on an excellent breakfast. Not one but two pretty girls had smiled at him as he made his way though the subway system and to the hidden APO headquarters, and both had looked sincere. Arvin Sloane was in his office with the door closed, and someone had brought in doughnuts, which meant that Marshall had been able to scoop up an extra jelly-filled without feeling particularly guilty.

At the water cooler, Eric Weiss had offered up a new joke about *Star Trek* fans, and Marshall had understood the punch line without feeling insulted. Marcus Dixon had asked him to thank his wife for the tuna casserole she had prepared for lunch the day before and he seemed to mean it. Everyone in the office seemed happy, or if not happy, at least productively engaged with assignments that interested them.

Even better, each of Marshall's current projects was on track to timely completion. His workroom, nestled among files servers and workbenches, was a beehive of activity. Another attempt to reverse-engineer the firmware code wiped from the captured microwave pistol was proceeding apace, and if the results weren't what Marshall wanted, at least he knew that he was on the right track. Another computer was busy modeling communication satellite orbits and associated signal footprints, and possible combinations thereof. The glue on his newest pop-up book had dried nicely, and the results were quite satisfactory. Marshall hand-made the interactive books as a heat sink for excessive nervous energy, and to enhance his hand-eye coordination, but this one had turned out so well that he was considering trying to market it commercially.

He pursed his lips and shook his head at the thought. It was tempting, but he would almost certainly have to submit it for security review, and there was no way that could be fun. It was so much more enjoyable to do his work and not have to deal with bureaucratic functionaries.

"Marshall?" Vaughn asked. His knuckles drummed on the open door in a courtesy knock. "Busy?"

"No, well yes, but busy-good," Marshall said. He tore his gaze from the monitor that detailed the stats of the firmware recovery effort. "Come in, come in. Is this about that, you know?"

Mid-evening the previous night, Vaughn had called him at home and asked a favor. That had been a surprise, if a welcome one; he liked the young field operative, but rarely had contact with him outside of work. The favor had been basic stuff, just some vector-progression on a scanned photo, but Vaughn had thanked him profusely.

Vaughn shook his head. "No," he said. "But that was good work, Marshall. I appreciate you doing it on private time."

"Aw, it was nothing," Marshall said. He had a harder time with compliments than insults, for some reason. He drummed his fingers nervously, then realized he was probably being rude. "Doughnut?" he asked, presenting the paper plate eagerly. "I've got an extra."

"No, thanks," Vaughn said, leaning against the door frame. He looked sufficiently tired that even Marshall noticed. His eyes were bloodshot and shadowed.

"You know what's good for jet lag?" Marshall asked. He set the doughnut-laden plate aside and opened a workbench drawer. Inside were a soldering iron, a pair of protective goggles, several electronic diagnostic wands, a set of hex nuts and half a dozen pill bottles. He grabbed one and showed it to Vaughn. "B-1 complex," he said. "That, and plenty of fluids."

Vaughn smiled. "No thanks," he said again. "I'm fine. It's not jet lag. I was up late with Sydney."

"Oh." Marshall was never sure what to say to things like that. To cover his confusion, he looked away and returned the bottle to its hiding place. He liked Sydney and he liked Vaughn and he liked them together, but he didn't like to talk about it.

The doughnut seemed to call to him.

"It's not like that, either," Vaughn said as casually as he might have commented on the weather. Marshall envied him that confidence. "We had some stuff to talk about, and then I took her to the airport."

"She okay?" Marshall asked. He knew better than to ask about an operative's activities, but he felt a twinge of worry. "She's seemed—I dunno, tired lately."

"She'll be fine, I think," Vaughn replied. He answered the unasked question, too. "She'll be back later. But enough of that. I brought you something."

From his pocket, Vaughn took a small plastic bag with a Ziploc seal. On the bag, in his neat handwriting, were a date and a time. Inside the bag, visible through the transparent membrane, was a twin of the button-size information tap that Sydney Bristow had recovered from Washington. "Take a look at this," Vaughn said, handing it over.

"Where?" Marshall asked eagerly, sure that he already knew the answer.

"Cuzco," Vaughn said in confirmation. "The local police were kind enough to sell it to me. They recovered it from the gallery."

The doughnut forgotten, Marshall opened the

evidence bag and examined the tap. It seemed intact. With rapid, practiced movements, he locked into a miniature vise on his workbench and removed its cover. He ran the appropriate pair of leads from an integrated data reader and pressed them to either side of the tap. Vaughn was watching him with a quizzical expression.

"Induction makes 'em adhere," Marshall said. "The same way they read the in-board GPS." He flipped switches and tapped keys. "This takes a few minutes. Alcatena used a pretty slick data compression algorithm that—"

"I don't need to know all that," Vaughn interrupted.

No, of course he didn't. Flustered, Marshall shifted mental gears with conscious effort. "These things have miniature GPSs in them, and they record audit trails for their transmissions." He typed more commands into the computer terminal he was using. A schematic world map appeared on the monitor screen, overlaid with a latitude-longitude grid.

"You said before that you couldn't backtrack," Vaughn said, but he sounded hopeful.

"I couldn't," Marshall said. "Not with just one."

He pulled up the satellite-track model he'd been running. "At least, I didn't think I could, but I was trying. But now that I have two signal points—"

"You can triangulate?" Vaughn asked eagerly.

"Kind of. It's more complicated than that, really," Marshall said. He paused. "But, yeah, I can triangulate, sort of. I think."

Triangulation was a mathematic technique that was essential to telecommunications. Essentially, for a three-point network or sub-network, knowing the loci of two points enabled the determination of the third. It was an underlying principle that enabled the world's geosynchronous satellite positioning (GPS) network, and had been used countless times in strategic surveillance.

The exercise confronting Marshall now was a bit more complex. The little information taps worked not by sending information directly to its ultimate destination, but via an elaborate store-and-forward sequence using multiple satellites as relays. He had hoped that the satellite track modeling system he'd kludged together would compensate for that extra complexity.

This was exactly the kind of problem he enjoyed most. With a single known point and some guided extrapolation it might have been possible to determine the data's destination—possible, but very difficult. With two data points, however, there was no "maybe" about it.

"Piece of cake," Marshall said as numerical values scrolled across his screen. Without taking his eyes from the monitor, he grabbed the remaining doughnut and began to eat. Powdered sugar dusted his chin. The world was a happy place.

"Um, Marshall?" Vaughn asked.

"Huh? Yeah?" he said.

"Is this going to take long?" Vaughn asked patiently.

"Oh. Oh, no. Couple minutes at the most," Marshall said. For a moment, he'd forgotten that other people's minds worked differently from his. Not better or worse, necessarily, but differently. Possibilities and issues that he found obvious weren't nearly so evident to his coworkers.

He pointed at the information tap and the leads that linked it to his bench hardware. "The connection's fast, but it could be faster. The more info I can pull out of this, the more I can work with. It's like, better bit rate means better image resolution." He set his post-breakfast treat aside and tapped the monitor, indicating a fuzzily drawn orbital track that the software had drawn on the displayed map. His finger left a drop of jelly on the membranous screen. "Here," he said.

The track had snapped into focus. It was a low, elliptic orbit. The red loop ran in an offset vector that covered most of the world's continents.

"That cover's a lot of territory," Vaughn said dryly.

Marshall tapped another key. Three red stars appeared on the map. Beside each was a callout that presented latitude and longitude coordinates, specific to nine figures.

"There they are," Marshall said, and tapped the screen again. "D.C., Cuzco, and, uh, Sweden."

"Good," Vaughn said. He patted Marshall on the shoulder. "I've got some calls to make."

WASHINGTON, D.C.

Mornings were when it hurt the worst. The doctors had explained why. Something about the first part of the day, when the body was shifting gears from sleep to wake mode, did things to the nervous system. Plus, the early hours were when the previous night's medication lost its last efficacy as the body's elaborate chemistries finished processing the painkillers to nothingness. The nerves came back online, the pills and shots went away, and the pain came back, with a vengeance.

But before it did, and just as she woke, there were moments when Keisha Wyatt was happy to see the sun's rays shine through the window of her hospital room. As sleep gave way to wakefulness, she felt a kind of eerie tranquility. It was as if she were suspended between two worlds, and neither could claim her completely.

The monitor at her bedside chirped. Just wakening, she noticed it. As the day wore on, she knew, she would not. The piece of equipment chirped every five seconds, here and in the nurse's station down the hall. One of the doctors had told Keisha the chirp was the sound of life, and that she should value it, but she couldn't. She had heard the bright electronic noise so many times that she scarcely heard it at all anymore.

She was staring blankly at the ceiling, trying to collect her thoughts and waiting for the hurt to begin in earnest, when the door to her room opened. That was a surprise. In the days since her emergency surgery, hospital life had fallen into a predictable rhythm. Doctors' rounds, visits from family, meals, and physical therapy sessions all had their own assigned bits of day. Those were the hours she had to share. The first minutes of the day were hers and hers alone.

Her caller was a young white woman, trim and attractive. She had chestnut hair pulled back in a bun, and she wore a doctor's white coat. Keisha was reasonably sure that she had never seen her before.

"Hi," the woman said as she realized that Keisha's eyes were open. "Did I wake you?"

"Who're you?" Keisha asked. Even to her ears, the words were a bit of a slur. If any of her kids had spoken so sloppily, she would have chastised them, but here and now, it was the best she could do.

"A friend," the lady doctor said after a moment. Her voice was low and soft, but carried well. "I just wanted to see how you are."

The lady doctor moved to the diagnostic monitor and read something on it. There was a clipboard chart hanging at the foot of Keisha's bed and she looked at that, too, reading and nodding. When she looked up, she wore a slight smile that made her look years younger.

"Well, from what I can tell, you're doing better," she said, and now her voice was brighter.

"Doesn't feel like it," Keisha said. The dull throb in her shoulder was less dull now. "D'you have my pills?" she asked.

The doctor shook her head. She checked the chart again. "The nurse will be by with your medication in, um, twelve minutes." She paused. "I'll be gone by then," she said.

"Huh?" Keisha asked fuzzily, still not fully awake.

The woman came to her bedside again. She leaned close to Keisha, close enough that Keisha could see the worry in her eyes. Something about her face was familiar. She had good skin and strongly drawn features, and a good hairline that framed her large, expressive eyes well. She looked like a model or an actress, and Keisha wondered where she could have seen her before. "Do I know you?" she asked, speaking a little bit more clearly now.

"No," the doctor said.

"Who are you?" Keisha asked a second time. She wondered if she was still asleep and dreaming. The medicine did that sometimes.

Feather-soft, the doctor's fingers stroked Keisha's hair. When they grazed her forehead, the touch was cool.

"No, we don't know each other," the visitor said. "In some way I don't understand, part of me thought we did, but we don't."

Keisha didn't understand, but she wasn't yet sufficiently awake to mind not understanding. The fog that clouded her thoughts had not yet retreated completely.

"I looked at your chart," the woman continued. "You're going to be all right."

"Hell, I knew that," Keisha said. People were always telling her that she was going to be all right. Even after a night's sedated sleep, she was tired of hearing it.

"You've got a titanium steel pin in your upper arm and a grafted artery, but you're going to be all right," the woman said. She could have been speaking to herself, for all the notice that she gave Keisha's response. "You're going to be all right." She said it like a mantra.

"I *have* seen you before," Keisha said. Her eyes narrowed. A remembered image drifted up from somewhere in her memory. It was of a woman who looked like this one, but with darker hair and skin. She had been a Latina, and she had worn a utility worker's uniform instead of a doctor's white coat. "Was it at—at the office?"

Her visitor smiled at that. She leaned close again and kissed Keisha's forehead. "Hush," she said. "Sleep."

When the nurse arrived with her pills, Keisha asked who the new doctor had been.

"New doctor?" the nurse said blankly.

LOS ANGELES

The briefcase was black leather with brushed aluminum trim. As men's accessories went, it was neither outmoded nor trendy, but had the kind of classic lines that never went out of style. Beneath its leather skin was an inner shell of tempered tool steel, three-eighths of an inch thick and tough enough to block most small-arms fire. The frame was still heavier metal, with reinforced hinges and an electronic locking system. The monogram on one side read A.S.

Arvin Sloane took a last look at the case's contents and nodded before closing it. The locks engaged with a sharp and simultaneous *click!,* and their tiny LEDs flashed red. He was not by nature a particularly expressive man, let alone one given to theatrical gestures, but he looked profoundly melancholy as he surveyed his surroundings. His computer was powered down, the "in" basket on his desk was empty, and the coffee service that sat on a side table was empty and clean, awaiting its next use.

He hefted the case and looked toward his office doorway just in time to see Jack Bristow step into view.

"Going somewhere, Arvin?" he asked. He glanced around the office, taking the details in quickly before returning his attention to Sloane.

"Jack," Arvin said. Melancholy gave way to surprise, and then to reserved composure as he looked up at his visitor. "I was going to speak with you about this."

"I doubt that," Jack said. He closed the door behind himself and then settled again into Sloane's guest chair. "But if you wanted to talk to me, here I am."

"Actually, I was on my way out," Sloane said. "Will you walk with me?"

Jack shook his head. "No," he said. "Sit. We need to talk."

"Is it about Sydney?" Sloane asked.

Jack shook his head again. "No. Now, sit, or I'll make you sit."

"Threats, Jack? I'm surprised."

"No. Not threats. Just a simple statement of fact," Bristow said. "We need to talk, and now's the time." He paused. "Who's in Sweden, Arvin?"

Sloane stepped to the side table. He checked the coffeemaker's basket, positioned the beaker, and pushed the switch. The warm scent of brewing coffee filled the air. "What are you talking about, Jack?" Sloane asked. He seemed fascinated by the brewing coffee.

"Let's look at each other while we talk, shall we?" Bristow said. "I think that I've always afforded you that courtesy."

Sloane shrugged and returned to his desk. "Very well." He glanced at his watch. "I have a few minutes. Explain your question and I'll see if I can answer it."

"I just spoke with Vaughn," Jack said. "And he just spoke with Marshall. They're working on more detailed reports, but the short version is, the signal tap Sydney found in D.C. sent information to an address in Sweden."

"It sounds to me like you know more than I do," Sloane said. "About this situation, at least."

"I finished reviewing those documents I recovered when I secured the pistol in Virginia," Jack continued. "Deal memos, delivery instructions, that sort of thing. They don't say anything we didn't already know, but how they say it is interesting. Several phrases seem direct translations of idiomatic Swedish." He paused. "I was right, by the way. The Russian arms were payment for delivery services. I don't think the Blue Mountain Boys would have been permitted to use the micro guns."

Sloane nodded.

"But I was," Jack continued. "I think it's a trail of breadcrumbs. I think we're being led somewhere, and Marshall says it's Sweden, so I will ask you again, Arvin. Who's in Sweden?"

"I believe Nadia is," Sloane said. A look of real sorrow crossed his features. "I know that she is," he corrected himself.

Ten seconds passed in silence, then twenty. Finally, Jack took a deep breath and said, "I'm sorry, Arvin. I won't ask how you know, but who has her?"

"Hildebrandt."

"You told us he was dead," Jack said.

Sloane leaned back in his chair, and the ghost of a smile flickered across his features. "Haven't many of us been 'dead' before?" he asked. "Add one to that number, then."

The armored briefcase still lay on Sloane's desk. Jack drummed his fingers on it. The metal plate inside rang like a muffled bell. "And you were going to deal with this situation yourself, weren't you?" he demanded.

The coffee was ready. Without comment, Sloane walked back to the side table. Even after his cup was full, he continued to grasp the decanter with one hand. Jack watched him carefully as steam rose from the vessel.

"Don't do it, Arvin. Don't try to stall any longer, and certainly don't try anything physical. I'm much better at that sort of thing than you are, and I'm not in the mood," Jack said. "I told you, we need to talk."

"Fair enough," Sloane said. He set the decanter down again. When he returned to his seat, he left the cup of coffee behind too.

"I'm not going to ask just what it is you were planning to do," Jack said. "You're smart enough to know that paying ransom never works, and I don't think you'd try a solo attack. Turning yourself over to him also seems a bit unlikely."

"You said you weren't going to ask," Sloane said coolly.

"Look, you know why APO is configured the way it is," Jack said. "Checks and balances. Some of us like it and some of us don't, but we're a team again. You've got to let us in on this."

"Sydney. So nice that you could join us," Arvin Sloane said from the head of the table.

She nodded as she took her seat in the APO briefing room, slightly embarrassed and more than a little surprised. Sloane was not a humorless man, even if she found very little about him funny, but sarcasm was not something he did well.

"I'm sorry I'm late," she said. She was tired and a little stiff from the long trip to D.C. and back, but she felt good about the way things had gone. "I had some personal business that needed attending."

"We can't let personal business interfere with our operations," Sloane said, but he delivered the rebuke mildly. "No matter how enticing. We have other priorities to consider."

Sydney watched him carefully. Something about Sloane was different today. The faint fidgeting she had noticed before was gone. She could still see concern and worry on his tired features, but something else colored his expression. After a moment, she recognized it as a look of resignation. Anxiety stabbed at her.

"Has there been any word on Nadia?" she asked. Again, she felt an unaccustomed sympathy for him, despite their history. For all of Sloane's many and manifold flaws, he seemed to love his daughter. Regarding Nadia, at least, his concerns and Sydney's ran in close parallel.

Sloane surprised her again. In fact, to judge by the others' expressions, he surprised almost everyone at the hastily convened meeting. Only Jack Bristow, her father, showed no reaction to what Sloane said next, and she had to wonder why.

"Yes," Sloane said. "She's being held in Gevalia, Sweden. Specifics will be provided to you with your operational instructions, but Eric will give us a brief overview now."

"Who has her?" Sydney asked sharply, before Weiss could commence.

"Some thirty hours ago, I received a clandestine communiqué from someone purporting to be Burton Hildebrandt," Sloane said. "He also purports to have Nadia in his custody."

"You told us he was dead!" Sydney said. Anger swept away her fatigue. Thirty hours was a long span in her fast-paced life. If she took Sloane at his word, more than a day had passed since Hildebrandt had made contact. Sydney's mind raced. She thought of how much progress might have been made, how many leads might have been missed. This was not merely discretion on Sloane's part, but something close to betrayal. She said, "If we'd known the truth—"

"We operate on a need-to-know basis, Sydney," Sloane said. His words were firm even if the rationale was hopelessly insufficient.

"You mean, you lied to us," Sydney accused him. "You should have—"

"Sydney!" Jack Brisow interrupted. "It can keep. We're on a tight schedule here."

That was a surprise too. Jack Bristow defending Arvin Sloane was not a common event. Sydney wondered at his reasons and then shook her head slowly. There would be time for recriminations and justifications later.

"All right," she said. She glanced at Eric, who flashed her a brief, nervous smile. He looked like he was waiting for a bomb to explode, and Sydney realized that she was the bomb. "I'm sorry I interrupted," she said. She knew that Nadia's status must weigh heavily on his mind too.

"That's okay," he said, and stood. The briefing screen came to life. The first image was of what looked like a mansion or a lodge, two wings attached to a central structure. "This is the Zorn Clinic," Eric said. "It's an elite plastic surgery clinic, catering to the needs of the very famous." He paused to correct himself. "The very rich very famous," he said. "It was founded by one Emile Zorn, who used to be pretty famous himself. He died a few years ago, and ownership passed to other hands."

"Hildebrandt's?" Sydney asked, interrupting again, despite herself.

"We think so, Sydney, yes," Sloane said smoothly. "Please. Allow Eric to continue."

"Yeah, Hildebrandt," Weiss said. "Or someone who worked for him. All this happened around the same time as the, um, greatly exaggerated reports of the man's demise."

He clicked his wireless mouse. "Here's a picture

of him, by the way. Just in case," he said as the screen image gave way to another.

Sydney studied the new picture. It was of a stern-looking man with graying blond hair and gray eyes. "How do you know he's in Sweden?" she asked.

"We don't," Weiss said. "Not for certain. But we know someone is, and we know that it's likely the party or parties behind the arms deal. Marshall was able to backtrack and triangulate the signals from their comm equipment."

Marshall grinned, quietly pleased with himself.

"Whoever Alcatena was working for, whoever hired Muñoz, he's in Sweden at this address," Eric continued. "Now, I've been able to gather some logistical information that should be useful. . . ."

He continued in calm, businesslike tones, methodically laying out the patchwork quilt of data that he had pieced together from scores of sources. The specific identity of the person who had assumed control of the clinic was unknown, hidden in a thicket of banking regulations. Construction permits had proven more accessible, indicating that substantial remodeling had taken place in the clinic in the months following Hildenbradt's reported death. Finally, and most promising, Weiss had been able to make a tentative connection between shipments of exotic electronics equipment and the clinic.

"I can't be certain about this," he said. "But the clinic's main supplier of medical supplies has common ownership with an electronics firm that Hildebrandt favored. I think that one is acting as the other's proxy." He paused. "Questions?" he asked.

"Yes," Sydney said. She shot a glance at Sloane. "Who goes, and when do we leave?"

"I'll let your father handle that portion of the briefing, Sydney," Sloane said. He sighed heavily. "A word, though. This is not entirely a rescue mission, but one of apprehension. The microwave weapons are too dangerous to allow free commerce. Our superiors have directed that we make eliminating their source our first priority."

CHAPTER 12

SWEDEN

Perched on the Baltic coast near the River Dalälven, Gevalia was an ancient city with an appearance that only hinted at its full age. During the same decade that the American colonies had declared their independence of England, great fires had nearly destroyed Gevalia. The roaring blazes consumed most of the city, devouring wood-timbered churches and warehouses and homes that even then had been centuries old, reducing them in mere hours to cinders. Gevalia's present-day design was a legacy of that disaster. The city was an orderly grid of broad avenues and crossroads, accented by a generous scattering of recreational parks.

Surrounding Gevalia were farmland and wooded hills, and nestled in those hills was the Zorn Clinic, a surgical facility famous in certain very small circles. Housed within the facade of a fourteenth-century hunting lodge and founded by the surgeon Emile Zorn, the Zorn Clinic was a provider of state-of-the-art plastic surgery services. Among the relative few who had heard of the place, the Zorn Clinic's reputation was the stuff of legends. Zorn's management catered to the very rich and the very vain. Even to secure a consultation with an admitting surgeon required extensive behind-the-scenes maneuvering. The identities of those who came to Zorn, and the procedures they underwent, were carefully guarded secrets.

Doktor Thorsell had explained much of this with gentle patience. He was a portrait of Old World grace and style. He wore his gray hair in a short brush cut, and the tips of his neat mustache came up in waxed curls that might have looked absurd on most men but merely looked formal on him. His eyes were a shade that was common in northern latitudes, a shade of blue so pale as to look frosted, and framing them were crow's-foot wrinkles. They became more pronounced whenever he smiled, which was often. Seated behind the low desk in the tastefully appointed office, surrounded by framed diplomas and expensive furniture, he positively oozed concern and authority. It was a good look for a doctor, and the kind of look that would inspire trust in troubled women, especially.

"No, I assure you, Fröken Robbins," he said. He spoke English well, albeit with an accent, and his occasional lapses into Swedish seemed deliberate, perhaps done for emphasis. "Our discretion is absolute. Sweden's confidentiality laws are among the most strict in all the world, and the Zorn Clinic's policies are even more respectful of the privacy of our patients. We would not prosper, otherwise."

"You *do* come highly recommended," the young woman said, with a flutter of eyelids and long dark lashes. She could have been a player in a silent movie. The woman had a fair complexion, so nearly bone-white that she seemed never to have spent a day in the sun in all her life, with only traces of color on the cheekbones and lips. Her hair was matte-black. It had been styled with a single upswept curl at each ear, and bangs that hung low over her hooded eyes. "But this business is all so very embarrassing. If any of my friends should hear, I would never hear the end of it. Imagine, a Robbins having plastic surgery." She smiled wanly. "That's the *Massachusetts* Robbinses, of course," she said.

"Your secrets are safe," Thorsell assured her yet again. This was the third or fourth time he had made the promise, and now, at last, he had begun to sound a bit weary of it. "The Zorn Clinic's patients list includes some of the most prominent names in the world. We have an exclusive clientele, and we work very hard to maintain it. You may have utmost confidence in the Zorn Clinic."

The woman who called herself Valerie Robbins chewed her lower lip nervously, biting it hard enough to deepen it pale red. She half-closed her eyes, pressed the perfectly manicured fingers of one hand to her temple, and slowly nodded, making the expensive earrings she wore swing and sparkle. "I suppose you're right," she said. "I shouldn't have come so far if I had doubts."

Thorsell nodded. "If I may, please?" he said, and extended his hand.

Robbins reached into the large fabric purse

that she held in her lap. Reluctantly, she pulled out and handed him a large envelope. Rather than paper, it was made of plastic, thick and opaque, and closed with metal clasps. "Here's my personal file," she said. "My own doctors wanted to send it electronically, but I thought that was too risky. I didn't trust it out of my sight."

Thorsell waved one hand dismissively. "I could not access them here, at any rate," he said. His desk held no computer. "I prefer to work from paper goods. Your physicians seem to be very thorough."

In response, she rolled her eyes fetchingly. "*They* didn't want me to come, though. *They* said that surgery wasn't indicated. Imagine."

"Imagine that," Thorsell said.

She winced visibly as the doctor opened the envelope. "You *will* lock everything away somewhere safe, won't you?" she asked anxiously.

"Of course," the doctor murmured. "They will be perfectly safe."

"Really," Robbins said. She gave a ladylike shudder. "I don't like the idea of my file rubbing shoulders with other people's."

"Hmmmm," Thorsell said.

"It's my nose, you see. Since the accident, it's never been the same," Robbins said. "Do you need to know about the accident?" she asked anxiously. She seemed to be a woman who spent much of her life in a state of anxiety. She tapped the bridge with one finger. Her eyes went liquidly bright, and her voice caught. She seemed close to crying. "It used to be ever so much nicer, until the horse bolted and that branch hit me. I used to be *so* much lovelier."

Thorsell was only half-listening. He was deep in a review of the file she had provided him, examining X-ray films and hand-drawn diagrams, notes, and prescription histories. Without looking up, he said, "Your records will be seen only by the persons performing the procedure."

"Persons!?" Robbins asked. "More than one? Not just you?"

He didn't look up as he continued to examine the documents she had given him. "Of course," he said, sounding distracted. "Persons. Myself, the surgical nurses, the anesthesiologist, my students—"

She interrupted him. "No students!" she said sharply. "I will not be a learning experience!"

"No student surgeons, then," Thorsell said. He

looked at her seriously. "That will impact the clinic's fee, of course, and my own fee."

She laughed softly. "Of course," she said. She spoke with the easy assurance of the very rich, the calm dismissal of financial concern as trivial.

"Very well, then," Thorsell said. He took a compact viewer from a drawer in his desk and clipped one of the X-ray films into place. He looked from the ghostly image to his patient's profile and then back again, and shook his head. "I do not understand," he said. "In the films, the damage looks significant. I would expect it to be more readily apparent."

"Are you blind?" Robbins asked. "I don't want a blind doctor! I'm ruined! Ruined, I tell you!"

"From here, at least, it is scarcely visible," Thorsell said. He still smiled politely, but there was a puzzled look in his eyes.

"Don't *tell* me that," Robbins said petulantly. She stamped one foot. "Everyone tells me that, and I don't want to hear it. I don't pay people to tell me things I don't want to hear!"

"Just so," Thorsell said, with an air of weary resignation. Apparently, even a man accustomed to the complaints of the very rich had his limits.

"Allow me to examine the defect more closely."

Robbins was ensconced in an armless ash-wood and leather chair before his desk. Among the very few concessions that the office made to its function as a consultation room was a small, padded stool on spring-loaded casters. Thorsell rolled it to a convenient position beside her and sat. He took a pair of plastic gloves from his pocket and donned them.

"With your permission," he said. When she nodded, he leaned close and used one index finger to trace the line of her nose. He had a surgeon's hands, at once strong and gentle, and his touch was feather-soft, barely grazing her skin. High on the bridge of her nose, where cartilage gave way to bone, he paused. "Odd," he said. He looked at her, thoroughly confused now. "There seems to be no damage here at all. Are you certain that you provided me the correct films?"

As he spoke the last words, Sydney's arm snaked under his, and her hand found the back of his neck. She jabbed him there once, quickly, with the tiny hypodermic needle that she had palmed when taking the envelope from her purse. Thorsell's eyes widened in surprise, then rolled back in their sockets as the drug took effect.

Sydney caught him as he fell and lowered him gently to the deeply carpeted floor. She pressed two fingers to his left wrist and counted slowly. The pulse was slow but steady. She nodded, reassured. The physician would be unconscious for at least an hour, to recover with no side effects. Her scheduled appointment with him had nearly that long to run. She stepped to Thorsell's now-unoccupied desk and verified that his intercom phone was set to "Do Not Disturb."

She wished he'd had a computer. With direct access to the clinic's network, things might go more easily. She might even have been able to find information on Nadia. There was no use crying over spilt *mjölk*, though. Other possibilities remained.

Sydney upended her purse. The remainder of its contents spilled onto the polished wood surface of Thorsell's desk. The most important of them were a tightly folded nurse's uniform and accessory props. Sydney changed clothes quickly, then used a cosmetic sponge to remove the alabaster makeup that she had worn as Valerie Robbins. A few quick passes with comb and brush and her antiquated hairstyle fell away, too, collapsing into a looser coif that looked longer. She perched the uniform's white cap on her head and removed her earrings.

She glanced in a mirror. Valerie Robbins was gone, and in her place was an anonymous member of the Zorn staff. The transformation wasn't complete, but it would suffice. No one would recognize her as the wealthy prospective patient. Hopefully, the uniform she wore would encourage others to look past, rather than at, her, especially if she took reasonable care not to draw attention to herself. She donned a pair of heavy, horn-rimmed glasses from the complement of equipment.

"Phoenix to Merlin," she said softly. As she spoke, she opened the file drawer in Thorsell's desk and began reviewing its contents hastily. One after another, she opened and glanced at dossiers. "Do you read?"

"Merlin here," came Marshall's familiar voice. She felt the words as much as heard them. The heavy temple bars of her spectacles hid audio pickups and miniature speakers that worked by bone induction. If she spoke aloud, however faintly, Marshall would be able to hear her words.

"We've got a problem," she said. "No network access from this office."

"He doesn't have a computer?" Clearly, Marshall found the idea unimaginable. Sydney found it hard to believe, herself.

"Nope," Sydney asked. "Not here, anyway. Have you found a backdoor?"

"Not yet," Marshall said. "But I will."

At her feet, Thorsell had begun to snore softly. With a grimace of disgust, Sydney closed the file drawer again. None of the faces or names had been familiar. There was no information on Nadia here, either. It had been too much to hope otherwise.

"Any directions?" she asked. As she spoke, she reversed her handbag so that the former lining became a new exterior. With quick, assured motions, she folded her civilian clothes and stowed them neatly inside the reversed purse.

"I'll see what I can do," Marshall said. He hummed a little tune, and Sydney could hear his fingers tapping keys in the background. The communications equipment was really quite good. "Back," he said after a moment. "Infrastructure configuration shows a lot of activity in the east wing. Lots of information processing, lots of power distribution. I think that's where you want to go."

"Okay," Sydney said. The original plan had

been to access the network using in-house assets, and review floor plans and room directories. That wouldn't work now.

"There's a lot of signal interference, too," Marshall said. As if to illustrate his point, the background static surged to new levels, then subsided.

"That could be clinic equipment," Sydney said. She thought of X-ray machines and positron-emission tomography scanners and other high-energy diagnostic devices.

"Nah, this is something different," Marshall said. "The waveforms are wrong." He paused. "There's probably an armory on premises, or at least some kind of testing facility."

"Thanks," Sydney said. She glanced at Thorsell, still unconscious on the carpet. "I'm going to have a look around. Be ready to move."

"Will do. Keep in touch. Merlin out."

Thorsell's office had two doors. One, Sydney knew, led to a private elevator and the building's lobby. Valerie Robbins had used it to enter. The other was to the clinic's working areas. It opened onto an anonymous, pristine hallway that could have been taken whole from a facility anywhere in the world. Spotless white walls defined a softly lit corridor that ran for long distances to her right and left. She recalled what Marshall had said and turned eastward.

The Zorn Clinic lay far enough outside Gevalia to ensure reasonable privacy for staff and patients but close enough for ready access to the city and commercial transportation. Privacy and seclusion had been further ensured by careful landscaping so that the place was surrounded by rolling hills and strategically placed trees, as well as a weathered stone wall. The sky above was a cloudless blue and the air was crisp and cool, but not cold. Summers in this part of Sweden were temperate.

Just beyond the clinic gates, parked beneath a sheltering oak, were two vehicles. One was a pearl-gray Mercedes with diplomatic plates. The other was a black utilitarian van, with a small, dish-shaped radio antenna mounted on its roof. On the van's side was the famous emblem of a major telecommunications provider, and under that were the words FÄLT FORSKNING, Swedish for "field research."

Inside the van were Marshall and Dixon.

"She's in," Marshall said. He leaned forward

from his backseat lair and passed a headset to Dixon, seated behind the van's steering wheel. "She's on and she's on."

Dixon accepted the headset. He listened for a moment before responding. "A lot of hum," he said.

"I'm getting a fair amount of interference," Marshall said. The back of the van was half-filled with electronics equipment, including five computer monitors. One was mounted in a jointed framework. As he spoke, Marshall turned it so that Dixon could see it in the rearview mirror. "Here," he said. "Take a look."

They had spent some hours before dawn on the Zorn grounds, mapping the place's security cameras even as they placed surveillance equipment of their own. Marshall's screen displayed a video feed from one of his cameras, showing a heavy, stolid building with granite-faced walls and a high-peaked roof. It looked like a hunting lodge, with a central hall and two flanking wings.

"There," Marshall said. "Nice, huh?"

Dixon looked in his rearview mirror at the monitor's reflected image and nodded. "Like a post-card," he said patiently.

Marshall said, "That's the close-up. Here's the

extreme close-up." He tapped some keys. The feed image vanished, replaced with a multilevel diagram of the clinic's interior structure. He had constructed the image using construction plans commandeered from local government offices. "Now, for my next magical trick," he continued.

The surveillance equipment included not only cameras, but remote electromagnetic resonance imagers. Refinements of devices in use at United States airports, they could read power sources at a reasonable distance. When Marshall brought their inputs online, the computer diagram became exponentially more complex. The building's internal wiring, telecom, and computer networks were indicated as a maze of computer-generated lines in different colors. Marshall identified them one by one, then pointed at a blob of light that glowed green in the clinic's east wing.

"Interference," he said. "That's the primary source. I can't resolve the image in any greater detail, but I bet that's what we're looking for."

Dixon turned in his seat to get a better view. Even with Marshall's guided tour, the annotated schematic was confusing in its complexity. "Where's Sydney?" he asked.

"Second floor, west wing," Marshall said. "Here. I'll show you."

He entered some more commands, highlighting a section of the computer model and then expanding the area he had selected. Viewed in greater detail, the multilevel diagram became easier to understand. Hallways, rooms, staircases, and even elevator shafts were clearly rendered, even if the images were still minimalist in execution. Moving along one of the corridors was an indicator of Sydney's progress, a bright yellow circle with a wedge-shaped section missing. The gap opened and closed as she made her progress.

Dixon looked at Marshall. "Clever," he said in a way that suggested he didn't think it was very clever at all.

"Hey, Phoenix," Marshall said into his headset microphone, happily oblivious to Dixon's expression. Ordinarily, Dixon would have held down this end of the operation, but given the nature of the support Sydney needed, Marshall got to have most of the fun this time. He paused for her response. "I think you want to head east," he said. "East and down. I'm getting a lot of interesting readings from there."

Dixon looked at him quizzically. Marshall changed the screen view again. Now, it presented a less-detailed view of the entire structure, still with the wiring diagram overlays. Elaborate and detailed throughout the Zorn Clinic, they became a tangled, clotted mess on the lower levels of the east wing. "Yeah," he continued, for both Sydney's benefit and for Dixon's. "Lots of power consumption, lots of stray EM radiation. I think that's the jackpot. Anything worth checking into is probably there."

No one seems to like hospitals, and Sydney was no exception. She had infiltrated such establishments before, with mixed success. The most recent such expedition—her visit to Washington—was still fresh in her mind. Experience proved there was a generic similarity to such institutions, and familiarity was good. It made her job easier.

All hospitals and clinics, from the least to the most expensive, had certain things in common. Typically, the staff moved with confidence and focus, even if what they were focused on wasn't readily apparent. Staff might dawdle and loiter at nurses' stations and medicine lockers, but in the hallways between, they tended to glide past one another with only the briefest of glances, if that. Appropriately attired personnel, in nurse uniforms or surgical whites or the colored scrubs of support staff, were effectively invisible unless they did something to draw attention to themselves. Most hospitals, even the most exclusive, had turnover rates sufficient that a new face would likely go unnoticed. To avoid eye contact was to avoid confrontation.

Those ingrained mores served her well as she made her way from Thorsell's office toward the western wing of the facility. Doctors passed her, scarcely taking notice. Orderlies wheeling file carts made way for her without making eye contact. Clad in white and drifting along spotless white corridors, Sydney felt a curious sense of detachment that was unusual for an undercover assignment such as this one. She felt like a ghost in a world of ghosts, with only Marshall's disembodied voice to keep her company.

This, too, was familiar. The sense of déjà vu was strong enough to be constant but not enough to dull her focus. As she strode past the open door of a patient's room and heard the chirp of a diagnostic monitor, she realized why she felt as if she had been here before.

She could have been in Washington again, in the hospital, leaving Keisha Wyatt's room. Even with the higher-tech, more modern, surroundings, the underlying resemblance was there.

Sydney pushed the thought from her mind, smiled at an orderly, and continued her exploration. If she could get to the lower levels without being detected, perhaps she could identify what Marshall could not.

CHAPTER 13

Ingrid Dirks accepted the blue-jacketed file folder from Hans, the flunky from Administration who had been tasked as the substitute interdepartmental mail deliverer this week. She cursed softly in her native Swedish. The other on-duty nurse looked up from filling out a report form at the workstation they shared. She looked at Ingrid with a question in her eyes, then nodded in understanding as she saw the folder.

"That Hans!" Ingrid said. "Can't he get anything right?"

File folders were color-coded to identify patient status. Orange folders held comprehensive case histories, covering the period from initial admission through final discharge. They were for use by doctors on call, physical therapists, nurse practitioners, and nurses like Ingrid. Files in orange folders were welcome at the nursing station. Blue folders were not.

Blue folders were for initial consultations and came under the cognizance of the admitting physicians. Blue folders held confidential information on people who had not yet formally become Zorn patients, and those people tended to be individuals who valued their privacy greatly. Nurses weren't supposed to have access to blue folders or their contents, at least not before those contents had been redacted and sanitized for use in their orange counterparts. This was the fifth blue folder that Hans had delivered in error to Ingrid's workstation in as many days. She was becoming quite annoyed with his inattention to even the most basic of management protocols. "I'll take care of it," she said. She would have liked to have taken care of Hans instead.

"I can, if you want," the other woman said. She

had a lower, softer voice than Ingrid's and a faint German accent. She was copying numbers from one sheet of paper to another. "Just wait a moment, until I have finished here."

"Nej," Ingrid said sharply. "I don't want this here." She glanced at the adhesive label on the folder and the name neatly printed here. "It's one of Thorsell's," she said. "I'll take it to him now."

Her coworker indicated the appointment calendar that hung behind them, next to a poster illustrating proper exfoliation techniques. "Thorsell is busy for the entire afternoon," she said. "He has a new patient."

"This will only take a moment," Ingrid said. Once, early in her tenure at Zorn, she had peeked inside a blue folder. The ensuing reprimand was still an unpleasant memory. "I don't want this here," she said again.

"Thorsell doesn't like interruptions," the other nurse warned, then noticed that Ingrid was already on her way. She sighed and focused anew on her work.

Ingrid had other reasons for wanting to make the disposition herself. After a slow morning of mostly administrative work, the opportunity to stretch her legs was too enticing to ignore. Her sensible flat shoes were quiet on the tiled floors as she turned right, then left, and headed east toward Thorsell's office. As she passed a third patient's room, she noticed another nurse coming toward her, handbag tucked under her left arm. She was wearing the clinic's standard uniform and signature cap, but Ingrid didn't recognize her. She was an attractive woman with black hair and good skin, but she seemed to have unfortunate taste in eyewear. The heavy horn-rims she wore did nothing for her features. Ingrid decided that the stranger was probably new staff, perhaps from another floor. Whoever she was, she moved confidently and with great self-assurance.

"Hallå," Ingrid said in polite acknowledgment as they passed each other.

The woman smiled and nodded, but said nothing and did not pause in her progress. Instead, she worked her way east briskly, in the general direction of the elevator. Ingrid wondered silently which floor she worked on. The thought didn't last long. She had other matters to concern her.

Thorsell's office was at the end of the second hall. He was one of the clinic's most prominent surgeons and had been assigned a consultation room befitting his status. Ingrid took a deep breath and knocked on the door. No one answered.

Ingrid looked again at the folder and at the name on it, and then back at the unyielding door. If she interrupted Thorsell at his work, she might be reprimanded again. But if someone saw her in possession of a blue folder, worse might happen.

She knocked again, then gripped the door handle and turned it. "Excuse me, Doktor," she said, opening the door. "Excuse me, I am so sorry to interrupt, but . . ."

Her words trailed off into silence as she saw the dignified man who lay unconscious on the thickly carpeted floor. A moment later she had dropped the blue folder and was kneeling at his side. It took only a moment to verify that he was breathing and that he had a strong pulse, and only a moment longer to find the telltale hypodermic puncture on the back of his neck.

Ingrid's hands trembled as she snatched up the telephone receiver and dialed the switchboard, but her voice was steady as she spoke. *"Hallå?"* she said. "Connect me to Security. I am in Thorsell's office. Someone has attacked him!"

* * *

"User by user, the Swedes make up one of the ten top markets for wireless communication," Marshall commented. He had a tendency to pepper his conversation with technical factoids. It was his idea of small talk. "They use it for everything," he said. "Telecom, data transfer, Internet, banking, the works. That makes this backdoor thing a lot easier."

Dixon only half-listened. He had turned frontward in his seat again, and his hands gripped the van's steering wheel loosely. He was wearing a comm-link headset, tuned to the coded signal from Sydney's eyeglasses. He had assumed the base station role partly to have something to do and partly because Marshall's attention was divided between Sydney and more technical matters.

The APO technical expert was still comfortably ensconced in his nest of electronics. Four of his five monitors presented his computer model of the Zorn Clinic from various angles and in varying degrees of detail. Marshall glanced at them in turn with consistent frequency, but the majority of his attention was directed at the fifth.

It showed another computer-generated model, a graphical user interface that resembled a control panel. The imaged panel was divided into a dozen segments, four columns of three. Each of them included futuristic-looking switches and buttons that had been imaged in enough detail that they looked tangible and real. Each of the twelve was further adorned with an identifying label. ELEKTRICITET, LIVSVILLKOR, ALARM, INFRASTRUKTUR, FINANSIELL—the names were in Swedish, many of them tantalizingly familiar. At the bottom was the steadily pressing line of a status bar, with a rapidly incrementing percentage value next to it.

"Almost there," Marshall said cheerfully. He smiled. He was a man who liked systems that worked well. "I've downloaded the system protocols and rewritten the security overrides. The application should finish compiling right about—"

He paused. On his screen, the now-complete status bar flashed as the number beside it grew a third digit, to read "100 percent." In rapid succession, the twelve panels of Marhsall's virtual command center relabeled themselves.

Electricity. Environment. Alarms. Infrastructure. Financial. The names were all in English now. The monitor image looked like controls for a computer game devoted entirely to the mundane.

"—now!" Marshall concluded. "We're in. I'm

in, I mean. They don't know it, though. But they will. I'm in control of, um, ninety percent of the primary in-house infrastructure systems. That's everything that's accessible by wireless. I control the horizontal, I control the vertical," he said. "I can't get at everything, but I can get at a lot."

"That will have to do. I'll tell her," Marcus said. He opened his headset mike. "Phoenix, do you read?" he asked. He paused for her response, then continued. "Merlin has opened the backdoor and is reaching inside." He paused again. "Do you read? You're breaking up."

"Maybe if I run her feed through some filters, it'll help," Marshall said. He looked at a locator screen again. Sydney's signal had moved much closer to the glowing knot of interference indicated in the eastern section of the clinic, but the yellow circle that represented her had lost much of its definition. Marshall did something to the keyboard and then shook his head. "Nothing I can do at this end. She's right on top of things. And it's going to get worse before it gets better."

"You're breaking up, Phoenix," Dixon repeated. "You're on track, but if you go any farther, we'll lose contact. Do you read?"

Somewhere in the complex assemblage of receivers, processors, and monitors that shared the back of the van with Marshall, something buzzed. With an abrupt look of concern, he turned from the locator screen to the complex virtual command center that he had so painstakingly assembled. One segment flashed red now. "Uh-oh," Marshall said softly.

Marcus looked at him, then at the screen, his stolid features alive with concern. "What is it?" he demanded. "What's happened?"

"Someone just scrambled Security," Marshall said. He indicated the appropriate screen section. "They might be onto her. Or onto something."

"Phoenix," Dixon said again, with greater urgency this time. "Hello? Hello? Damn!"

"Damn?" Marshall said in a small voice.

Dixon tore off the comm-link headset and tossed it aside. "She kept going," he said. "Dropped right off the world."

From the unoccupied seat beside him, Dixon snatched up his jacket. He climbed quickly from the van and donned the garment, running his hands quickly along its expensive-looking fabric to smooth away any wrinkles. From an interior pocket he retrieved tinted aviator glasses, and driving gloves made of leather that was as limp and sheer as silk. Donning them, Dixon abruptly looked very well-to-do, indeed.

"I'm going in," he said, settling behind the wheel of the Mercedes parked beside the van. The precision-engineered motor roared to life. "Give me seven minutes and then give *them* hell."

"Uh," Marsall said. "Yeah, sure."

Sydney was within eyeshot of the central elevator bank when the twin metal doors whisked open and two armed men emerged. The holstered guns they wore weren't the little microwave guns, but thoroughly conventional-looking automatic pistols. They looked quite deadly, nonetheless. The men wore brown and khaki uniforms, each with a gold badge on his breast pocket. They looked professional, but they didn't look like police. Her immediate guess was that they were hospital Security, and it wasn't hard to guess why they had been summoned.

She dropped back and ducked into the open doorway of the patient room she had just passed. She half-closed the door quickly and quietly, and peered through the opening that remained.

"Who are you?" someone asked in Spanish. A middle-aged woman lay in the room's single bed, her face swathed in bandages. The magazine she held in one hand fell to the floor as she demanded Sydney's identity.

"No Spansk," said Sydney, who actually spoke Spanish quite well. She shrugged and mimed speaking, then shook her head. *"No Spansk,"* she said again. She shrugged and grinned in a manner that she hoped was endearing. It was easier to sidestep the question than to try to answer it convincingly.

The woman stared at her in outraged bafflement. Clearly, she was not accustomed to being ignored. Sydney didn't care. She returned her attention to the hallway.

The guards were no longer alone in the lobby. The nurse Sydney had encountered earlier had found them and was explaining something. The nurse gestured and pointed down the same hallway that had led Sydney to the elevator lobby. One of the guards said something to the other. All were speaking so softly that Sydney could hear only the occasional word.

One of those words was "Thorsell."

As if on cue, a voice sounded in her glasses frames. "Phoenix, do you read?" The words were distorted and clipped, as if barely punching through a barricade of static. Sydney had to listen carefully to understand them.

"I'm here," she said, still focusing on the hallway conference. One of the guards was trying to soothe the nurse. She wished that all of them would go away.

"Merlin has opened the backdoor and is reaching inside." He paused again. "Do you read?" came the response. "You're breaking up."

"I hear you," Sydney said, very softly. She cupped a hand over her mouth so that the words would not carry.

"*Qui etes-vous?*" the room's occupant demanded, asking her identity in French this time. If possible, the second language made her sound even more imperious. Her eyes flashed from behind the mask of bandages.

"*No Fransk,*" Sydney told her, trying very hard to sound polite. It was another lie, and a less believable one. The majority of educated Swedes spoke a second language, and many of those spoke French. It was unlikely that staff serving the international clientele of a medical facility would speak neither Spanish nor French. She hoped that the patient wouldn't try Portuguese next.

The guards were gone now. Something had gone wrong. Either Doktor Thorsell had recovered ahead of schedule, or someone had found him. Either way, management knew that something was afoot.

"You're breaking up," Dixon repeated. "You're on track, but if you go any farther, we'll lose contact. Do you read?"

"Outrigger?" Sydney asked. "Hello? Hello?"

There was no answer.

"Dammit, miss, who are you?" the patient asked, in perfect English this time. "Who are you and what are you doing in my room?"

"I'm sorry, ma'am. I don't speak English. I'll have another attendant see to you shortly," Sydney answered, and darted back into the hallway.

The coast was clear now. She summoned the elevator and pressed the key labeled KÄLLARE, Swedish for "basement." Her headphones remained silent as the elevator cage moved quietly downward.

CHAPTER 14

Tires squealed as the pearl-gray Mercedes roared up the Zorn Clinic's driveway. They squealed more loudly as the car screeched to a stop that straddled pavement and walkway. The tall black man behind the steering wheel half-pushed, half-kicked his door open and climbed out, keys clenched in one hand. He wore a Savile Row–tailored suit and he moved with the dangerous grace of a jungle cat. Even as his Italian loafers struck the flagstone walk, an attendant in valet's livery appeared at his side.

"Hallå!" the uniformed man said. *"Välkommen!"* He gestured at the mis-parked car with one hand and extended the other for its keys.

The driver shook his head angrily and brushed the valet aside, half-toppling him. He ran up the broad stone stairs three steps at a time, without any apparent effort. The entrance to the clinic building was flanked by two more uniformed attendants and he brushed past them, too, and opened the heavy oaken doors without their help.

The clinic's reception area looked less like a lobby than like the trophy room of the hunting lodge that the place had once been. Ten or so remarkably well-dressed visitors sat on stolid, traditional couches and chairs, or conferred with staff in huddled groups. The carpet was thick and rich. Heraldic plaques and mounted-game trophies decorated the oak-paneled walls. The black man ignored all of that and charged to the receiving desk.

"Where is she?" he roared. He pounded on the desk and glared at the woman who sat behind it.

"Hallå?" she asked tentatively. *"Välkommen?"* She was radiantly attractive with sparkling eyes and delicate features. Presumably, her assignment

to the front desk was intended to advertise the quality of the clinic's services.

"Where the hell is my wife?" Dixon thundered. He pounded on the desk again.

The lobby background chatter, never prominent, faded away completely. Prospective patrons and other callers broke off their own conversations and redirected their attention to the angry man who was making a scene. The reception clerk suddenly looked very worried.

"Please," she said in halting English. "I must ask—do not speak so."

"I'll speak as I damned will please," Dixon snarled. His voice dropped numerous decibels but became more ominous. "You've got my wife in this scalpel farm of yours and I want her back, right now!"

"Your wife—she is a patient?" the receptionist asked.

"My wife, she is trying to spend more of my money," Dixon snapped, mocking the woman's slightly singsong accent. "When I got back to the hotel, she was gone and there was an appointment card for this place. Now, I want to see my Valerie, and I want to see her now!" He leaned close to her as he spoke the final words.

"Your name?" she asked. She looked genuinely frightened now.

"I am Lionel Robbins," Dixon said imperiously. He sounded as if he expected her to recognize him. "Of the Massachusetts Robbinses."

The seated woman's fingers trembled noticeably as she picked up her telephone and dialed. A moment later she murmured something Swedish into the open line. As she spoke, she watched Dixon nervously, like a bird might watch a cat.

"Speak American, dammit," Dixon muttered, but broke eye contact with her. He looked around the reception area, looking back at the people who were looking at him. "What the hell," he said, still testily, still in character. "Haven't any of you ever seen an angry husband before?"

The receptionist had continued her low-pitched conversation in Swedish. Now, she said, "Ah. Doktor Thorsell?" Then her face fell. She returned the receiver to its cradle.

"What is it?" Dixon demanded, his voice rising again.

"Something has happened," the woman said. She trembled as he glared at her. "Your wife had an appointment with Edric Thorsell, one of our finest specialists, but there has been—" She paused and swallowed noticeably. "There has been an incident."

"Incident?" Dixon asked. He looked ominous, but a close observer might have noted a flash of concern in his eyes.

"Please, be seated," she said. "Someone will—"

The door behind her opened. A blond man in a business suit stepped through it, right hand extended. "Hello, Mr. Robbins," he said. He smiled, revealing teeth more numerous and more perfect than any man's should be. "I'm Karl Witka," he said in flawless English. "I'm with clinic Public Relations. Why don't we step through here and talk?"

"You really have very lovely features," the doctor said. He leaned closer to Nadia as she lay in the bed. He wore a magnifying loupe, monocle fashion, and held a small light in one hand. He was carefully studying the play of shadows that the light created on her face. "Very symmetrical and expressive," he continued. "You must have been very popular."

"Been?" Nadia asked. She didn't like hearing herself referred to in the past tense. "Why are you doing this?" she continued, without trying to resist him. Still securely bound to the bed's frame, there was no way for her to elude his attentions, and she had already learned how persistent her host could be. Better to endure him and hope for an opening.

It was as if he had not heard the question. Rather than answer it, he posed one of his own. "Do you know how many muscles there are in the human face?" he asked. His breath smelled of wintergreen, even through the surgical mask he wore.

"Eight major sets," Nadia said. She felt more tension than fear, but it was enough to make sounding calm a challenge. It was difficult to relax, or even feign relaxation, when tied to a hospital bed and being examined. She was not accustomed to being so powerless.

"Just so," the doctor said. He tucked the light into a jacket pocket. "They interact with remarkable complexity."

"You should know," Nadia said sharply. "You're the expert."

The doctor grasped her chin gently but firmly

with his left hand, and turned her face to present a three-quarter profile. With his right index finger he traced the line of her nose and then her cheekbones. His touch was curiously gentle, but dispassionate. He might have been examining a Greek marble.

Nadia considered trying to bite him, but decide against it. Her host had not come to the room alone this time. A burly man in a lab jacket stood by the door. Presumably, he had been assigned double duty as orderly and security.

This was only the second time that she had seen the doctor. Since originally awakening, she had been attended by nurses and orderlies, always in pairs. They had fed and bathed her and tended to her needs, but never spoken. The cumulative effect of the combined solicitude and silence was maddening in its own way. She had been almost happy when the doctor had made a return visit.

Almost.

The man looked at her in a way that was disturbing, and it was never worse than when he took the loupe from his eye and shook his head. His gray eyes were cool and dispassionate, like metal. "No," he said. "Surgery was not my original discipline. Even now, I have only an educated layman's expertise.

After some years of study, I can understand the efforts of others, or direct them."

Now, Nadia felt a sudden chill. She remembered the stimulant injection that he had administered. That action, coupled with his choice of wardrobe, had led her to assume that she was being held prisoner by a surgeon. "What kinds of efforts?" she asked slowly.

He looked at her. For the first time during this visit, his gaze met hers directly. "You are being held in the Zorn Clinic, Fraülein Santos," he said. "Tell me. Are you familiar with the establishment?"

Nadia blinked in surprise. He had told her where she was. He had given her not just a general location, but a specific name. That wasn't knowledge that she could reasonably expect to have, and still live.

Something had changed since the last interview.

"The world's foremost plastic surgeons contend to practice here," he continued, taking her silence as a negative. "The majority of the facility is devoted to satisfying the whims of the world's idle rich, but other work is done here, by a select and special staff."

He released her chin and leaned back in his

chair. Still gazing at her steadily, he continued. "Research into reconstructive surgical techniques, for example," he said. "Exceedingly complex, such studies require experimentation. Subjects are difficult to find." He turned to the assistant. "Schedule the X-rays for this afternoon," he said. "A full-spectrum cranial complement. I am only concerned with the face."

The burly man nodded.

"This is not a good idea," Nadia said, but even as she spoke, she knew that her words would not convince. "I have friends. Friends and *family.*" She emphasized the final word. For whatever reason, her captor seemed wary of Arvin Sloane. There seemed to be no harm in trading on that wariness.

"Nein," came the reply. "Arvin has failed to—"

Something buzzed. The man in the surgeon's mask stood and drew a wireless phone from his pocket. *"Yah?"* he said, and stood silently for long seconds as he listened. He said nothing to his caller when the conversation ended, but merely returned the phone to his pocket.

"There is a disturbance in the east wing," he said. "Probably of no import, but I must see to it. We will speak again before your surgery."

"Surgery?" Nadia asked. "What are you going to do!?"

He turned again to the orderly. "See to her," he said. "Report any developments to me immediately."

Then he was gone.

In the black van, Marhsall sat quietly. He liked listening to music while he worked on technical issues, but when assigned to surveillance work like this, he preferred to keep unnecessary sensory input to a minimum.

He had mounted a small clock on the van's interior wall. Its liquid crystal numerals flowed one into another silently. Six minutes and fifty-eight seconds had passed since Dixon had left him, then six minutes and fifty-nine seconds.

"Showtime!" he murmured as six at last gave way to seven. The agreed-upon waiting time had passed at last, with glacial slowness.

He pressed one finger to the cool glass surface, next to the words FIRE ALARM. The icon flashed red. Marshall nodded. "That should do for starters."

Instantly, another screen element flashed. "No, no, no," Marshall said. "Can't have you calling for reinforcements. No one needs to hear about your troubles." He tapped the screen again, and the second red flash disappeared. The connection between the Zorn Clinic and the municipality of Gevalia had been severed. The establishment's internal alarms could sound until the cows came home, but no aid would come from the city's fire department.

"That's better," Marshall said, for no one's benefit but his own. The index finger of his right hand drew a lazy spiral in the air, a curved track that ended when he tapped the screen a third time. It was time to see if the building's sprinkler system worked. Another icon flashed as the remote-control protocols engaged.

The sprinklers worked—or at least the building management software thought they did. Marshall shrugged, pleased. The glass screen rang with a metallic sound as he tapped icon after icon. One after another, he shut systems down, or disrupted their proper functionalities.

The more the merrier.

Elevators could be strategic challenges. Sydney didn't like them much. They were heavy metal boxes suspended in space. Riding them meant trusting your life to whoever maintained them, not only in terms of competence but also intent. Riding elevators made you vulnerable and severely limited your options, offering no cover to speak of. They made excellent death traps.

Despite that, they had a certain commonality that was always welcome. They almost always had four walls, a handrail, and a control panel, and this one was no exception. But for the Swedish labels, she could have been in the telecom building in Washington again.

The control panel light slid down behind the buttons to illuminate one floor number after another. Suddenly, the car shuddered and came to a halt. Sydney wanted ten long seconds for the doors to open.

They didn't. Instead, a small light flashed on the control panel, positioned above a card reader slot. She understood instantly. Access to this floor demanded special authorization. She opened her purse again and took out the electronic pass-card override that she nearly always carried. It fit perfectly into the slot, and the doors slid back with a chime to reveal another, smaller elevator lobby. In its center was a guard station, manned by a slender fellow with a wisp of mustache. He looked up in shock as Sydney exited, and reached for his weapon.

She took two long steps and then a third one that transitioned to a leap, and threw herself over the desk at him. She slammed into the guard. Driven backward by the impact, his wheeled chair came to an abrupt halt against the wall, with Sydney pinning him in place. "Be very quiet," she commanded in Swedish. "Hand me the gun. Butt first."

He was trembling as he complied. The pistol he surrendered was one of the little microwave guns, almost identical to the one Sydney had seen in Los Angeles. She accepted it with a nod and curled her finger around the trigger-button.

"Please, no," he said as she trained it on him. "You have no—"

"Don't move," she said.

"This is a secure area," the man said. He was plainly frightened, but determined to do his job. "You should not be here."

"Shut up," Sydney told him again. Training the pistol on him, she said, "I know what these can do."

Now, the guard was terrified. He nodded obse-quiously and said nothing.

Sydney glanced at the security station's half-dozen monitors. Most showed absolute chaos. Hospital staff and patients swarmed through darkened corridors as fire sprinklers rained down on them. Marshall had initiated his diversion, she realized. That meant that Dixon was probably on the premises too. "Where is this?" she asked, indicating the screens.

"West wing," the guard said, trembling. "East wing, too, but upper floors."

She glanced at the ceiling lights, still bright and steady. "What about these?" she asked. "And the surveillance cameras? Why are they working?"

"S-secondary power source," the guard said. "M-more secure."

"Tell me," Sydney demanded, "are there any guests on this floor? Any prisoners?"

He shook his head, but his eyes showed that he was lying.

Sydney gestured with the gun. "I know what these things can do," she said again. "Now, tell me."

"Just one," he said. "A woman."

"Tell me where," she said. "In fact, tell me everything."

CHAPTER 15

Immediately past the lobby door was a small security desk with a uniformed guard. Witka waved Dixon past it and down the hallway that followed. Dixon watched him carefully for an opening as the friendly man led him to a small office, presumably his own.

"Let's go in here," Witka said pleasantly. Everything he said, he said pleasantly. His English was perfect, but had the artificial, trained sound of a radio announcer.

"Is Valerie back here?" Dixon said. He sounded

at once angry and slightly embarrassed. "I want my wife, and I want her now."

"So we gathered," Witka said. Rather than sit behind the office's desk, he dropped into one of the two guest chairs in front of it and gestured for Dixon to take the other.

"Look, I'm sure you people do fine work here," Dixon said in conciliatory tones. "But my wife doesn't need it, and I don't need the expense. I told her that a dozen times."

"Of course," Witka said, studiously nonconfrontational. "Can I interest you in coffee? We have an excellent custom blend."

"No coffee," Dixon said. "All I want is Valerie."

"Hmm. Valerie Robbins," Witka said. His desk held a computer and small printer. Without rising, he stretched one arm and plucked a sheet of paper from the printer's hopper. He looked at it as he spoke. "Yes. I checked the records. Mrs. Robbins checked in earlier for her consultation with Dr. Thorsell."

"She doesn't need any surgery," Dixon said doggedly. The office was small and nicely appointed, but windowless. Obviously, Witka's priority had been to get him out of the more public reception area.

That was good. He was inside the clinic's working area now, and privacy worked both ways. "I don't want her spending any money. All she talks about is her nose and you people. Her nose is just fine, dammit!"

"I'm sure it is," Witka said. "Please, Dr. Thorsell is very prompt. You wife will complete her appointment in—"

With a rumbling, spitting noise, water gushed from the office ceiling. It rained down in an oscillating spray, drenching both men. Witka yelped in stunned shock and said Swedish words that were presumably curses. The paper he held disintegrated. A fire alarm sounded in the adjoining corridor.

The torrent surprised Dixon, but not nearly as much as it surprised Witka. He had been expecting something and was ready to take advantage of the opening. His fist came up in a short, sharp arc, a trajectory that intersected with Witka's chin. The public relations flak yelped again and then fell silent. His chair toppled backward, dumping him onto the floor.

Without a second glance, Dixon rose from his chair and opened the office door a crack. Outside was bedlam. The fire sprinklers there had erupted as well, and the hallway now bore a passing resemblance to a public sidewalk during a summer cloudburst. Professionally attired men and women scurried instinctively for cover that did not exist, chattering at one another in panicked tones. The tide of humanity flowed in the general direction from which Dixon and Witka had come, where a flashing sign read UTGÅNG— "exit."

As Dixon joined the throng, the ceiling lights failed and emergency lamps came on. It had to be more of Marshall's work, and its effect was immediately evident. The staff redoubled their efforts to evacuate, focusing on the way out.

No one seemed to take any particular note of the big American who worked against the tide, heading deeper into the building. No one seemed to notice the pistol that he had drawn from a concealed holster either.

The burly man remained in her room after the doctor left. He stood by the closed and locked door, watching her without comment. Nadia had no doubt that the doctor's final murmured command had been to keep an eye on her.

She looked at him and smiled. He didn't smile back.

Nadia recalled that her masked host had uttered a stray word or two of German during his examination of her. It was worth a try.

"Guten Tag," she said, to no response. She tried Spanish, French, and half a dozen other languages. None of her greetings prompted any kind of reaction. Clearly, he heard but chose to ignore her.

It was time to try harder. She made herself looked worried, then made herself hiccup. That prompted a concerned expression on the guard's broad features, so she upped the ante. The ersatz hiccups became more violent, then segued neatly into ragged choking noises. Nadia's entire body shook, and she struggled convincingly against her bonds. Her mouth hung open and her tongue lolled back, as if she were in the thrall of seizure.

That did it. Concern gave way to something like panic as the bulky guard surged to her bedside. He bent over her, one hand at her wrist to check her pulse. The other tentatively reached for her open mouth.

When Nadia could feel his breath on her face, she struck. Making the fullest, best use of what little mobility she had, she rammed her forehead into his as hard as she could.

It hurt like hell, but it hurt him more than it hurt her. Caught completely by surprise, he slumped across her, unconscious.

Nadia's head hurt and red-rimmed holes danced in her vision, but consciousness remained. She strained against the bonds that tied her to the bed rails and managed to extend the fingers of one hand under the guard's jacket.

The soft restraints tying her to the bed were resilient plastic. Nadia had tested them repeatedly during her waking hours. The more she pulled at them, the stronger and tighter they seemed to get. They were impossible to tear, but should cut fairly easily. Given enough time, almost any implement should be able to do the job.

Inside the orderly's jacket was a pocket. Inside the pocket was a pen. It wouldn't have been her first choice, but it was the only one she had. Patiently, she uncapped it and bent her wrist back on itself, so that she could jab and dig at the restraint.

All she needed now was time.

CHAPTER 16

According to the briefing that Dixon had received from Weiss, the Zorn Clinic's patient population was approximately one hundred persons at any given time. The staff was slightly more than that number. It seemed to him now that every one of those two hundred personnel was swarming the hallways, moving hastily for the exits.

Most didn't seem to realize or care that he was an intruder, but by sheer brute force of numbers, they made the going tough. The flashing lights and sprinkler spray didn't make things any easier. He had to thread his way through a wave front of support staff and patients, many of whom required assistance. For an establishment that specialized in cosmetic and plastic surgery, Zorn seemed to have a high population of the wheelchair-bound, as well. He knew that the evacuating horde was comprised of civilians, or nearly so, but it was difficult to treat them with the consideration they deserved.

A nurse with an instrument tray came at him, too panicked to realize that he was blocking her path. He stepped aside. A waif-like girl in a hospital gown and with bandaged features tugged at his sleeve, demanding something in a language he did not understand. He tore free of her and continued. A security guard confronted him, hand on a holstered pistol, and ordered him to halt. Dixon dropped the man with a single slapping blow and continued on his way.

Through it all, he kept his eyes open for familiar faces. Sydney was somewhere in the building, he knew. Presumably, Nadia was. Even Burton Hildebrandt's august visage lingered in his mind's eye for easy reference.

Ahead was the building's central elevator core. Lighted signs flashed above each set of doors, blinking in time to the fire alarm's beat. No doubt, the signs warned not to use elevators in times of fire or emergency. Dixon ignored them and pressed the call button.

Nadia pulled against the restraint, hard. The remaining strands of spongy plastic snapped and her hand came free, at last. The awkward angle of her work had made her fingers go numb and clumsy, so she needed almost as long to free her second hand. That done, she wriggled free of the unconscious guard who still lay atop her, and climbed from the bed.

The world lurched crazily. Nadia maintained herself in excellent condition, but days of immobility had an effect on even the best muscle tone. She stumbled as she examined the room quickly.

There was little that she hadn't already seen from her bed, but that little was welcome. In the closet, she found the clothes that she had worn on the Peru assignment. By the time she finished donning them, most of the sensation in her hands had returned, and so had her motor control. Even her slight vertigo had dissipated.

She turned the guard over on his back and searched him quickly. His jacket pockets surrendered a pass-card, another pen, and a cell phone. His trouser pockets held a wallet and a clasp knife. Nadia permitted herself the luxury of glancing at it for a second. The small blade would have made cutting her bonds infinitely more easy, but there was no time to consider such things. After verifying that the guard was unconscious and likely to remain so, she stepped out into the hallway.

She took the knife with her.

Sydney had a second hypodermic needle in her purse, a twin of the one she had used on Thorsell. After finishing her interrogation of the guard, she used it on him. He lost consciousness almost instantly. She propped him up in his chair and headed down the corridor he had indicated.

The lower level of the clinic was vastly less complicated than the upper floors, but impressive in its own way. A single central corridor formed the spine of the complex, with sealed security doors and an occasional side-passage spaced along its length. According to the security guard, the facility's "special guest" was at the end of the hall. Unlike upstairs, this level seemed deserted. Presumably, the workforce had been summoned to deal with the events that Marshall had created.

She moved down the hall slowly, the commandeered energy pistol still in one hand. Halfway to the end, she decided that it was time to start checking the rooms' contents. Supposedly, one held Nadia. Certainly, others would hold persons or items of interest.

One by one, she opened them with her skeleton key card. The first three were simple storage, with crates and cases labeled in Swedish. The fourth was some kind of classroom, with chairs and a wipe-board and worktables.

The fifth was an arsenal.

Sydney inhaled sharply as she saw the room's contents. In one corner was a computer workstation, with chairs and monitors and a small workbench. The rest of the room was filled with metal racks, like bookcases. Each shelf held scores of the little pistols.

She stepped inside to take a rough count. Each rack had ten shelves, and easily twenty of the racks stood in the dimly lit room.

"Who are you?" someone asked from behind her. The voice was a rich bass, and the words were spoken with a slight accent. "Turn and answer me."

Sydney did neither, but she responded with a question of her own. "Burton Hildebrandt?" she asked.

"Who are you?" he asked again. "Another of Sloane's creatures?"

Another. Sydney savored the word. Nadia was here, somewhere. "He sent me," she said. "He wants to talk business."

"Fah. I think not. Not like this. I warned him," Hildebrandt said. "Now, turn. Slowly."

Sydney complied. The man in the doorway was tall and solidly built. He wore a surgeon's scrubs and mask. He held a microwave pistol of his own.

"Drop your weapon," Hildebrandt said. When the pistol fell and clattered onto the floor, he nodded. "Now," he said, "step closer."

Watching carefully for an opening, Sydney approached. After a few steps, he gestured for her to halt.

"Close enough," he said, studying her. "Another woman. Another Sloane daughter?"

The words were an accusation. "No," Sydney said sharply. "He is no father of mine."

"You work for him, then," Hidlebrandt said. His gray eyes flashed angrily. "An emissary. I want no emissaries."

"He wants to do business," Sydney lied. "We can offer a better price than—"

"Spare me your lies," Hildebrandt said. He backed up slowly, edging into the hallway. "Now. Come away from there, and we will speak of other matters."

She wondered why he wanted her to follow, and then realization struck: The guns and equipment behind her were likely vulnerable to microwave bursts. He didn't want to risk damaging his own wares. "We can talk here," she said.

"No. I would prefer not to fire in such close quarters, but I am fully prepared to do so," Hildebrandt said. "Now, come away and—"

Things happened very fast then, so fast that Sydney would later need to think carefully to remember their precise sequence. For now, however, instinct and reflex sufficed.

To Hildebrandt's left, Nadia Santos seemed to appear from nowhere. She threw herself on the doctor, smashing down on the wrist of his gun hand with a karate chop. Hildebrandt grunted in pain, but managed to keep his weapon. Nadia's other hand groped for his neck. It held an open clasp knife, the edge of which glinted wickedly.

"Nadia!" Sydney said.

Hildebrandt gave a cry of pain and tried to throw her off of him. He moved faster than Sydney would have expected, fast enough that he managed to break the other woman's grip on her weapon. It spun away, then fell to the floor.

Nadia clawed at Hildebrandt's face. The mask came away in tatters, revealing more tatters beneath. Hildebrandt's features lay in ruins. His face was little more than a mockery of how a man should look.

"Your father's work! Your father's!" he snarled, in pain and embarrassment. The hand that held the pistol came up and pressed it to Nadia's chin.

The knife was at his feet. Sydney flung herself to the floor without thinking, reaching for it. As if of their own accord, her fingers reached for and gripped the handle. Instantly, she found and assessed the blade's balance. The angle was difficult, maybe even impossible, but Sydney wasn't thinking about such things.

"Do not move," Hildebrandt said again. "Do not move or I will—"

Nadia's dark eyes found Sydney's. Their gazes locked. She made an infinitesimal nod.

With an absolute confidence that seemed to

come from nowhere, Sydney threw the knife. With unerring accuracy, it buried itself deep in Hildebrandt's shoulder. Now, at last, he dropped the pistol and fell, moaning softly.

He was still like that when Dixon found them, long minutes later.

After enough hours, the letters on the computer keyboard seemed to take on a life of their own. The keys seemed to take evasive action rather than subject themselves to the impact of Sydney's fingertips. Spelling suffered accordingly. Seated in her work area in APO headquarters, she leaned back and glared at the screen. She sighed and yawned, then laced her fingers together and stretched.

"Hey," Vaughn said, startling her. "Here." He handed her a tall container of coffee with a domed plastic top.

Sydney accepted it gratefully, but made a show of examining the trademark on the disposable cup's side. "Well," she said. "I know where you've been all morning."

He shook his head. He looked tired. His eyes were bloodshot and heavy-lidded. He took a sip of his own coffee before continuing. "No, you don't," he said. "I was consulting with Hildebrandt's intake team." He used the polite term for "interrogation."

"Oh." Sydney opened the coffee and took a sip. It was hot and good. "How's that going?"

"He sends his love," Vaughn said, with a wry smile.

"Uh-huh. I'm sure he does," Sydney said, and drank some more coffee. Slowly but surely, the world was becoming a brighter and happier place.

"He sure hates Sloane," Vaughn said.

"A lot of people do," Sydney said. She didn't feel like facing Vaughn when she said it, so she gazed at the computer screen instead. Now that fatigue had been pushed back, even a little, the words seemed to make more sense. She could see where to move this clause, how to rephrase that one. The work no longer looked hopeless.

"What are you doing?" Vaughn asked.

"Typing up some notes for the records," she said. "Sloane wants them by COB, and I'm leaving before then."

"Fun?"

"No," Sydney said. "Of course not. It's too much like homework." She drank some more coffee and looked at him again. "Really, Vaughn. How did the intake go?"

"About the way they usually do. It's like the five stages of death. First comes denial, then anger," he said. "Hildebrandt is at the anger stage now. But he's talking." He paused. "Mostly about Sloane," he said.

Sydney set down her coffee cup. She threw her hands up in mock disgust. "Okay, okay," she said. "I'll beg you to play the piano. Tell me about Sloane and Hildebrandt."

He smiled slightly. When he spoke, he drew out each word for emphasis. "It seems that our Mr. Hildebrandt and Sloane have a history."

"So?" Sydney asked. "They dated the same girl?" She regretted the words as soon as she said that. Sloane's role in her life, in her father's life, was a truth that fell uncomfortably close to the lame witticism.

Vaughn didn't seem to notice. "Nothing that

simple," he said. "It seems that Burton Hildebrandt was at one point in possession of a Rimbaldi page."

"Oh," Sydney said. The reference to the medieval visionary drove all thoughts of humor from her mind. Not so long ago, the pursuit of Rimbaldi's legacy had lent her life a nightmarish complexity. A rogue Arvin Sloane had been one of many contending for the pages and artifacts that Carlos Rimbaldi had left behind.

"Oh, indeed," Vaughn said. "But no more. Except maybe, up here." He tapped his forehead meaningfully. "In his noodle. Word is, it may even have been the basis of his rayguns."

"His life's about to get pretty interesting, then," Sydney said. To her surprise, she felt a twinge of sympathy. She had visited CIA-managed detention spaces many times in the line of duty. They were drab and cheerless. Inmates there were the targets of multiple CIA working groups and committees, each pursuing an individual agenda. Hildebrandt's alleged knowledge of Rimbaldi's legacy would make him especially in demand. It was almost certain that the Agency had his specific page in custody, but even so . . .

Vaughn seemed to have read her mind. He nodded. "Word is, we have the page he had. Sloane gave it to us."

That made sense too. The price that Sloane had paid to come in from the cold had been his cache of ancient artifacts and codex pages. It might also explain Hildebrandt's accusation.

"Your father's work!" he had told Nadia. "Your father's!"

If the microwave scientist had found himself without his source document, or with only a corrupted copy, the consequences might have been disastrous. She shuddered, however faintly, remembering the horror that had been hidden beneath the doctor's mask.

"How are you, Syd?" Vaughn asked, shifting conversational gears with practiced ease. "You look beat." He paused. "You look beat, but you look great."

"Thanks, I think," Sydney said. She looked again at the screen, then tapped a key. The appropriate security encryption protocols engaged, and the document saved and closed itself. She had done enough for now.

"I mean it," Vaughn said. He paused again. "I mean, how are you sleeping?"

"Oh. That." She knew that the question had

more than one meaning. She remembered his surprise visit to her apartment, the pizza, the long conversation. She even remembered the coffee ice cream she had been eating before he arrived, and why. "I'm fine," she said.

He looked at her, not doubtfully, but merely taking her measure.

"Really. I'm fine," she said. She gestured at her computer. "I came in early to work on this. If I look beat, it's because of the report, not—not the other thing."

Vaughn smiled. "I know," he said. "I just wanted to hear you say it."

"I like saying it," Sydney said. "Are you on for this afternoon?"

"I wouldn't miss it for the world," Vaughn replied.

Marshall Flinkman sat nervously. He was acutely aware of Arvin Sloane's steady gaze. He didn't particularly like being in Sloane's office. He was much more at ease in his own spaces, surrounded by the technological toys that he loved so much.

"No progress at all?" Sloane asked. The APO chief had summoned him for a private report, and the report wasn't going particularly well.

"Not none at all," Marshall said. His palms were sweaty, and he wiped them on the arms of the guest chair. "A little bit. But I haven't been working on it very long, really." He wanted to loosen his collar, but refrained. Someone had once told him that the action made him look like a cartoon character.

"Marshall, you've worked miracles in less time," Sloane said. He sounded mildly reproving.

"Yeah, but this is more than a miracle," Marshall said. "It's more complicated than I expected. The pieces of code that Syd—that Sydney—brought back aren't like anything I've ever seen before. I knew it was going to be hard, but now I know it's going to be harder." He laughed nervously. "Isn't it funny how that works?" he said.

He had spent most of the previous day reverse-engineering the firmware that drove the microwave pistols. The hardware would be simple enough to copy and mass-produce, but the operating system was proving to be a tough nut to crack. Many of the assumptions that Marshall had made based on his original review had proven wrong when considered in context with the data recovered in Sweden.

"I can do it," he continued. "It's just going to

take time." He paused. "Look, I knew that Hildebrandt was good, but no one's this good. The programming shows design breakthroughs like nothing I've ever seen before, except maybe—"

Sloane looked at him.

"Oh," Marshall said. He silently mouthed the name "Rimbaldi."

"Perhaps," Sloane said, voice uncolored by any emotion at all. "Would an interview with Hildebrandt help?"

"It might," Marshall said, "if he's willing to talk. But if he had anything to do with Rimbaldi, they've got him in a warehouse somewhere, surrounded by packing crates and stuff, like in *Raiders of the Lost Ark,* or *Citizen Kane.*" He grimaced as he remembered Hildebrandt's ruined features. The idea of interviewing the captured scientist was not attractive. "I hope they give the poor guy a mask or something."

"Why do you think he had made the clinic his base of operations, Marshall?" Sloane asked patiently.

"Oh. Yeah." Marshall blushed. When he was nervous, he spoke too fast, and lost control of the words sometimes. "To fix himself."

"No promises about the interview, but I'll see

what I can arrange," Sloane said. He turned his attention to his computer. "Please close the door behind you."

"I'll need a copy of that when you're done," Jack Bristow said.

"Huh? Yeah, yes, sure," Weiss responded. "I'm finalizing it now. Do you want hard copy or electronic?"

"Whatever you give Sloane will be fine. Just try to get it to me by tomorrow," Jack said. He hovered at Eric's shoulder, reading the screen. "Are you sure about the Russians?" he asked.

"Yeah." Eric rolled his chair back a bit to give the senior agent a better view. "The recovered data fits in with some background chatter Vaughn forwarded. K-Directorate had a contract in place for several major shipments, to be passed off to other parties unknown."

"The Blue Mountain Boys?" Jack asked.

Eric shook his head. "Just stoop labor."

"All right," Jack said with a nod. "Don't forget to copy me on that."

"It'll be done by COB," Eric said.

"Tomorrow's fine," Jack said. "I'll be out all afternoon."

The sedan rolled quietly along the wooded lane. The sun, shining through the sparse cloud cover, cast abstract shadows on the asphalt pavement before it.

"Sure you want to do this, Syd?" Vaughn asked.

"I'm sure," she said. "I should have done it a long time ago." She was wearing a simple black shift and had pulled her hair back into a simple fall.

A veil would have been too much.

"Are *you* sure you want to be here?" she asked. "You've had enough death in your life."

"I don't mind," Vaughn said. He corrected himself. "No, it's not that. I want to be here. Not just for you, but because I knew her too."

Sydney made a *hmm* of agreement and said nothing more until the car stopped in the parking lot of a small cemetery. When it did, she waved Vaughn away and opened her own door.

It was a beautiful day. The air was warm, but not too warm, and the cloud-flecked sky made perfect counterpoint to the painstakingly maintained landscape that surrounded them. Rolling green hills held white marble tombs and monuments. Except for the calls of distant birds, the air was quiet.

Sydney sighed. It was peaceful here. Her life was so filled with violence and intrigue that she sometimes seemed to forget how wonderful peace could be.

As Vaughn opened the trunk and took out the flower arrangement, a second car pulled into the space beside them. Sydney blinked in surprise as Dixon emerged from the driver's side. "Thought you could use some moral support," he said. "Hope you don't mind. I brought some company."

The "company" consisted of Nadia and, even more surprisingly, Sydney's father. His stern features looked gentle in the afternoon sun.

"The more the merri—" Sydney started to say, then caught herself. "No, no, I don't mind."

Dixon had been a guest in Francie's and her home. So had her father. And if Nadia had never met her predecessor, she was still family.

"I'm happy to see you here," she said. "All of you."

As the others exchanged pleasantries, Jack gestured to her to follow him for a private talk. Twenty or so feet distant, he spoke softly.

"Syd," he said slowly, looking vaguely uncomfortable now. "I'm not much for—for closure, but I think this is a good thing. I'm glad you worked it out for yourself."

"I'm not sure I did," she said, looking at him and then at Vaughn. In some ways, they were so much alike. "I think maybe I had some help."

The thought was still in her mind a few minutes later, when the small party rounded the last hill and came upon the marker that was their destination. It was a small, white stone, and above two dates, it bore a single name: FRANCINE CALFO.

It had taken a little bit of research to find the location, but only a little. Francie's body had never been recovered after her assassination. Her death had gone unrecorded until much later, but when the news had finally come, her family had acted on it. The stone was a memorial marker only.

They weren't the first to find it either. A small wreath lay before the monument. Puzzled, Sydney knelt and examined the note attached.

"Sympathies," it said. The only signature was a pair of initials. "A. S."

How had he known? The message was plainly for her. How had Sloane known that she would pick today, of all days, to pay her respects? The questions had no answer. She passed the note to Vaughn, who read it and scowled. She shook her head in warning before he said anything. This wasn't a day for anger.

"Hi, dear. It's taken a long time, but I'm finally here," Sydney said. "I'm so sorry that all this happened. I miss you. I know it's been years, but I miss you still, and I guess I always will."

The words hurt, but saying them made her feel better.

Pierce Askegren was born in Pennsylvania and lives today in Virginia, with many intermediate whistle stops along the way (his daddy was a railroad man). At various points in his so-called career, Pierce has been a convenience store clerk, bookstore manager, technical editor, logistics analyst, and writer for business proposals and industrial instruction materials. At one point, he knew an alarming amount about wireless communications protocols.

Pierce has written extensively for Marvel Comics characters, having authored or coauthored five novels featuring Spider-Man, the Fantastic Four, the Hulk, and the rest of the gang. His other previous series work includes *Gateway to the Stars*, a novel based on the popular *Traveller* RPG, and short stories featuring Marvel characters and TV's friendly vampire, Angel.